THE AMAZING ELVIS GOLD

THE AMAZING
ADVENTURES OF

HARRY MOON

WAND - PAPER - SCISSORS

by
Mark Andrew Poe

Illustrations by Christina Weidman

rabbit  publishers

The Amazing Adventures of Harry Moon - Wand-Paper-Scissors
by Mark Andrew Poe
© Copyright 2015 by Mark Andrew Poe. All rights reserved.

Rabbit Publishers
1624 W. Northwest Highway
Arlington Heights, IL 60004

Illustrations by Christina Weidman
Cover Design by Chris D'Antonio
Interior Design by Lewis Design & Marketing
Creative Consultants: David Kirkpatrick, Thom Black and Paul Lewis

ISBN: 978-1-943785-00-1

10 9 8 7 6 5 4 3 2

1. Fiction - Action and Adventure 2. Children's Fiction
First Edition
Printed in U.S.A.

Harry, I am going to break it to you
gently - having a friend like me
has consequences.

~ RABBIT

TABLE OF CONTENTS

Preface i

1. The Scariest Thing of All 1

2. The Terrible Name 21

3. Better Magic 29

4. The Sleepy Hollow Magic Shop. . . . 39

5. Sarah Sinclair 59

6. Rabbit 67

7. The Wand 77

8. Bad Mischief 89

9. Imagine 99

10. Saturday 115

11. The One Arm Vanish. 125

12. The Scary Talent Show 143

13. Loss 169

14. The Haunted Cube. 179

15. Monday 199

Author's Notes 207

PREFACE

Halloween visited the little town of Sleepy Hollow and never left.

Many moons ago, a sly and evil mayor found the powers of darkness helpful in building Sleepy Hollow into "Spooky Town," one of the country's most celebrated attractions. Now, years later, a young eighth-grade wizard, Harry Moon, is chosen by the powers of light to do battle against the mayor and his evil consorts.

Welcome to *The Amazing Adventures of Harry Moon*. Darkness may have found a home in Sleepy Hollow, but if young Harry has anything to say about it, darkness will not be staying.

THE SCARIEST THING OF ALL

There was plenty that was scary in Sleepy Hollow including the gloomy town square and the Headless Horseman statue.

At Sleepy Hollow Middle School, the students were the scariest thing of all. This seemed especially true around Halloween, when competitive heat ran high over who would win the Annual Scary Talent Show.

Harry Moon, an aspiring eighth-grade magician, would be a shoe-in for the win, as he was wonderful with table magic like card tricks, vanishing scarves, and pulling toy rabbits out of his top hat. But Titus Kligore, the school bully, had the resources and the sizzle to beat Harry Moon.

Last year, Titus and his buddies won the Scary Talent Show with a singing review of "Tonight We Party." They were only in seventh grade at the time, and they *still* won. Titus's guys, the Maniacs, were dressed in classic monster gear — The Mummy, Frankenstein, the Werewolf and Dracula - and their singing was pretty good.

Titus's dad, Maximus Kligore, was not only the mayor of Sleepy Hollow, but he ran the most successful costume shop in town — Chillie

Willies. Titus had had a big advantage over everyone else, since Chillie Willies had dressed Titus and his friends in the most outrageous, horrifying outfits that money could buy. Besides, everyone was afraid of voting for anyone else but Titus. Who wanted to be stuffed in their locker by the Maniacs?

This year, pain-in-the-butt Titus planned to win again with a singing revue entitled "Let's Get Hysterical," comprised of movie monsters — Freddie, Jason, Brain Eater, and the Saw. But there was a chill in the air. Word had gotten out that Harry Moon was out to win the competition, which made Titus and the Maniacs crazy mad. Tenacious and hard-working, Harry had been practicing his magic tricks every night after school in the Performing Arts Studio on campus.

3

Miss Pryor, the drama teacher who all the guys wished they could kiss, (rumor had it that Titus had planted one on her lips last year on her birthday) was in charge of the Scary Talent Show, and had told her class that Harry Moon was the guy to watch.

"One day," Miss Pryor said, "Harry Moon could be as good as Elvis Gold."

"Weooo!" said many in the schoolroom. The class was astonished by the teacher's praise. Elvis Gold was the most wonderfully magical magician in America. Just last week, Elvis Gold, locked in chains and frozen in a block of ice in the Hudson River, escaped certain death on screens all over the world. Harry had watched it dozens of times on his phone.

4

Titus Kligore did not enjoy hearing that Miss Pryor was glowing about Harry Moon. This meant competition for him. Titus was accustomed to getting his way and keeping control of the kids. He had to win the Scary Talent Show at any cost.

Titus Kligore had never liked Harry Moon one bit, which was not a good thing for Harry. Titus was huge — a good foot-and-a-half taller than Harry. He had a ginormous head and broad shoulders. He was one of the first guys to be able to make a really loud whistle without using his fingers by pursing his lips together in a peculiar way. He had learned that from his uncle, who, rumor had it, was in jail for stealing beer.

The worst of it was that Titus was reckless. His hormones were raging. He even had nine chin whiskers when he was in fourth grade. Now, he was wildly out of control.

The only thing Titus did have under control was the way he moved. He didn't walk through corridors like the other guys — he *swaggered.*

"Listen, runt," said Titus as he grabbed Harry by the collar outside the cafeteria. Titus slammed him against the wall. "I hear that Willow Wood is excited about you doing some smelly-butt tricks for them this Saturday night." Willow Wood was the old folks' home in Sleepy Hollow.

"That's funny," said Harry, wiggling out of Titus's grasp. "Because I'll be on stage here Saturday night beating the pants off you!" Harry's stomach was churning, but he refused to reveal his fear to Titus Kligore.

Harry heard a growl from over his shoulder as he hurried to his class. "You won't be on the Scary Talent Show stage if you know what's good for you." The growl had come from Titus.

❮∿❯

Daylight Savings time had kicked in, and it was dark when Harry Moon walked home from talent practice at the middle school. The wind was blowing, rattling the branches of the trees that lined the sidewalk. The wind was always stronger this time of year. The gusts shook the last leaves from the trees until the branches were bare, reaching out to the grey sky like fingers on skeletons' hands. The yellow moon drifted behind the shaking stick fingers like a nightmare unfolding.

Slish. Slash. What was that noise? Harry turned. Someone must be following him. But there was no one behind him.

It was almost Halloween in Sleepy Hollow, Massachusetts. Harry was a few blocks from his house. The wind was so intense that it even rattled the picket fences lining the many homes on Walking Dead Lane.

After Labor Day, the store fronts of Sleepy Hollow brought out the pumpkins, spider webs, witches brooms, and horror masks. Come Halloween, spooky stuff was big business. Times were hard everywhere, and Sleepy Hollow needed to survive. The town needed to amp up its spooky voltage to increase business.

For years, tourists came from across the world to discover the legendary Headless Horseman of the little town. He was the frightening, nogginless rider who had ridden over the bridge of Sleepy Hollow on a ferocious stallion, searching for a head to set upon his empty, bloody stump.

When the tourists could not find even a whiff of the ghostly horseman in the town, they left, disappointed. They had come to Sleepy Hollow, Massachusetts — the wrong frickin' state. It was actually Sleepy Hollow, New York they wanted. That was where Washington Irving's famous story of the headless horseman took place.

The tourists were sad when they learned the truth, and the town was losing business. It was a *lose-lose* situation. So Maximus Kligore, the mayor and Titus's dad, put a restoration program together to transform Sleepy Hollow, Massachusetts into "Spooky Town." The town even erected a statue of the Headless

Horseman in the town square. The statue, carved from the quarry rock in nearby Marblehead, stood a whopping fourteen feet high and had a steel ladder propped up against it. From Taiwan to Abu Dhabi, people came to the wrong town to have their pictures snapped on top of the horse, riding with the horseman who lost his head.

In the restoration, one little antique store was renamed I. C. Dead People'. A sundry shop on Elm Street was transformed to Nightmare on Elm Street. The garden tour became Spooky Tours. The harvest hayrides became Haunted Hayrides. A failing toy store was transformed into the popular Ghost Busters Shop. There was even a street renamed Magic Row, where spells, incantations, and magic tricks could be purchased.

All year long, the public school promoted scares. The wooden marquee in front of Sleepy Hollow Middle School proclaimed Home of the Annual Scary Talent Contest.

Over the years, Sleepy Hollow's fortunes

9

returned. Spooky became big business. The trademarked Headless Horseman Plush Doll, available in almost every store, was a sell-out at Halloween. Sleepy Hollow Cemetery was the resting place of some of American history's greatest thinkers and writers, from Henry David Thoreau to Nathaniel Hawthorne, but to most tourists, it was now the place where the fake Headless Horseman was buried.

Slish. Slash. There was that noise again. Normally, Harry Moon would be walking home from school with his buddies, Declan, Bailey and Hao, but he had stayed behind to practice for the big contest. He was alerted to the odd noise simply because it was out of the ordinary. It was not the knocking pickets or the whipping branches. It was the sound of metal scraping against metal.

Slish. Slash. He wondered how anything could see to follow him in this darkness, as the sky was dim and there were no street lamps on Terror Lane. Harry was very short for his age and seemed to blend closer to the ground than the sky. His hair was inky black and spilled from his head in every direction, making him look intense. The kids in his class called him "Einstein." It was his hair — he was smart, but not that smart.

Slish. Slash. As the sound of metal against metal grew closer, Harry walked faster. His backpack slammed against his shoulders. He picked up speed, but so did the sound. When the wind whipped at the branches making the skeletons in the trees seem to shriek, Harry ran. But his legs were short, and the follower's legs were not.

As if by magic, Titus Kligore was suddenly standing across from Harry Moon at the intersection of Nightingale Lane and Mayflower. Titus was huge compared to the diminutive Harry. Harry huffed and puffed as Titus stood, stoic. Titus was as steady and huge as the bronze Headless Horseman that graced the Sleepy Hollow town square.

"Get out of my way!" yelled Harry, as he tried to run around Titus. Titus leaned to his side, blocking his path. Harry went to the right. Again, Titus stopped him with his girth.

Slish. Slash. Harry looked down at the sound of metal sliding across metal. Even in the dim light, he could see the shine of the shears in Titus's hands as he opened and closed them. These were not paper or sewing scissors. They were *shears* — the kind used on farms to cut the wool off of sheep.

"What are you doing?"

"I've come to give you a trim," Titus said. His voice was dark and deep.

"Why would you want to do that?"

"Isn't your name Harry?"

"What of it?" Harry said, trying to dodge the tall Titus.

"Well, I have come to give your Harry Moon

butt a haircut," replied Titus.

"No way!" Harry cried, wiggling in Titus's grasp.

༄

Harry had suffered indignities with the double meaning of his name for a couple of years. He had thought the days of that ridicule were over. He didn't even realize there was a problem with his name until he was eleven when he and his friends were walking home from school. The Sleepy Hollow Booster Club bus drove by with a bunch of rowdy high schoolers headed to a football game in Lexington. It was on that autumn day that the older chaps pulled down their pants in the bus and stuck their naked butts through the open windows.

"Hey boys!" shouted the pranksters in the bus as the sixth graders gawked. "Here's something to look forward to!"

Harry and his friends laughed until their

13

sides split, not even fully understanding what was going on, as they watched the flank of eight bare rear ends waving from the windows, like a chorus line of dancers. A very unsettling sort of harmony.

"What do we have to look forward to?" shouted Declan to the busload of boosters.

"Your pink fannies becoming hairy moons, that's what!" a rowdy booster shouted back.

14

"Gross," replied Declan, wiping the image from his mind.

As the bus pulled away from them, fiery leaves of red and orange scattered in the exhaust's wake.

"What do you think that freak show was all about?" asked Harry as he kicked at the fallen leaves with his sneakers.

"Just stupid fools making a scene in the little suburb of Sleepy Hollow is all," answered Hao, the heavy one who swallowed Hershey's kisses whole with abandon.

"Ewwwee, pretty nasty!" added Bailey.

"That's adulthood for you," said Harry, with a sigh. "I just never wanna grow up and be like those silly fools."

"Yeah. Well — they seem to be calling for you, Harry Moon, to become a fool with them," said Declan with some snideness in his voice.

"Whaddaya mean?" Harry inquired.

15

"They seem to know your name, 'Harry Moon'."

"They were referring to their naked butts — not to me."

"I guess it's the same. I mean "hairy moon" or "Harry Moon?" said Declan. "Sounds like they are one and the same to me — just some real nasty, nasty bare-butt business."

"Ah, get outta here," said Harry. "That was *moonin'*. Everyone who is sophisticated knows about *moonin'*."

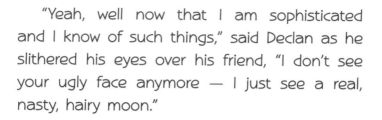

"Yeah, well now that I am sophisticated and I know of such things," said Declan as he slithered his eyes over his friend, "I don't see your ugly face anymore — I just see a real, nasty, hairy moon."

"I guess you're stuck with me," Harry admitted, throwing off the insults with a shrug of his shoulders.

"I am not stuck to you," laughed Declan, running with his red backpack bouncing on his shoulders. "I don't wanna be stuck to a hairy moon!"

"Me neither, Harry Moon," said Bailey, taking off after Declan. The two of them jumped up and flicked the branches of the maple trees as they ran, pushing the autumn leaves from the branches to make them fall faster than nature planned.

"I don't mind," said Hao, too uncomfortable with his weight to run. "Don't worry. They'll get over their nonsense by breakfast."

Sure enough, Hao was right. By the next day, with a new sun shining, as Harry walked to school, there were his buddies — Declan, Bailey and Hao — all waiting for him under the maple tree at the corner of Nightingale and Mayflower.

"Hey, man, we're sorry," said Declan. "We were just messing with you. We didn't mean it."

"That's okay," Harry replied as he walked with them.

17

"We just thought it was funny — that's all."

"It is kind of funny," said Harry, "and kind of ironic, too."

"How is it ironic?" asked Hao, who had spent the night on his cell phone, convincing his buddies they needed to apologize to Harry.

"It's ironic because I don't have a hairy rear."

"Yet," said Bailey in clarification. "Not yet."

They all laughed and "ewwed" at the thought as they walked down the sidewalk and away from the intersection.

Now, it was night. Two years later. The wind was howling and it was dark.

Slish. Slash. Titus towered over Harry. The clouds drifted past the yellow moon as the shadow of the sheep shears fell over Harry's face.

"Either you are going to drop out of the talent show, or I am going to cut off your hair, you Harry Moon butt," threatened Titus, as he leaned in and grabbed a chunk of Harry's hair.

Titus pulled Harry off the ground by his hair as Harry screamed in pain. *Slish. Slash.....* went the sheers as Titus chopped off a clump. No longer suspended by his hair, Harry fell to the sidewalk. As Titus threw the hair onto the ground, Harry Moon scrambled to his feet and ran for his life.

Titus turned and chased after him. Pulling his backpack from his shoulders as he sprinted, Harry swung it backward like a medicine ball at Titus's big head, knocking him to the ground. Harry ran as fast as his short stride could carry him. Before Titus could rise again, Harry was already down the street, disappearing into his own front yard.

20

THE TERRIBLE NAME

"You gotta let me change my name!" howled Harry.

Harry sat with his parents at the dinner table, facing his chicken and rice pilaf.

"No one is changing their name around here," said John Moon, Harry's father.

"Trust me, Harry, I have tried," said his ten-year-old sister, Honey Moon. Honey had straight blonde hair. Her bright, green eyes shone beneath an always-worried brow. "Every time I turn around, someone in home room is making a crack about me kissing or making out."

"At least they're not cutting your hair off," growled Harry, as he grabbed at his missing hair.

22

"No one will notice," said Honey Moon, unhelpfully. "You never comb it, so who will ever know? It looks just fine. Be happy your name isn't Honey or Harvest."

Honey looked over at her little brother, Harvest Moon, as he sat on a booster chair at the table.

"What's wrong with my name?" asked Harvest, as he plopped his hands into the apple sauce.

"It's a lovely name," said Harry's mom, Mary

Moon. "It's like a wonderful poem."

"It is a wonderful poem," Honey Moon added, "except if he grows up fat like Hao Durkin, and then everyone will be on his case...'Have another cheese wheel, Harvest. Hey, Harvest, have you had enough corn on the cob?"

"What's fat?" asked Harvest as he spooned apple sauce into his mouth.

"I need to legally change my name to Finn or Milo!" said Harry in a pleading voice. "And I need to do it before Saturday! That's the night of the talent show." Harry opened his arms as if imagining a dream. "Can't you see it, Dad? Can't you see it, Mom? 'And now... ladies and gentlemen...from Nightingale Lane, presenting his amazing magic, the one and only Milo Moon!' That sounds awesome, don't you think?"

24

"No, I do not think so," said John Moon. "We Moons do not back down just because of some little adversity."

"Little adversity?" Harry replied. "I was attacked with sheep shears!"

"How many times have we discussed your name?" John said with a kind, but firm, manner. "You were named after Harrold Runyon and you will carry his name with the same nobility as he carried it."

"Yes sir," said Harry glumly.

"You just have to rise above name-calling," said John Moon.

Harry Moon knew it was going to be another losing battle. During the Iraq War, John Moon's best army buddy was a man named Harrold Runyon. Harrold was a gregarious, gum-chewing, wise-cracking, got-your-back kinda fellow. From the age of fourteen, Harrold worked summers as a lifeguard at the Leisure Time Pool in Kansas City, Missouri. That's what Harrold did. He saved scrawny girls and boys from drowning.

When he was eighteen, Harry Runyon saved John Moon from dying, too. In Iraq, he took a bullet in the heart for his bud-dy. John grieved for his army friend, threw the first shovel of dirt over his coffin in Missouri, and vowed that he would keep his friend's memory alive. So when John and Mary Moon had their first child, they named the boy Harrold in honor of John's friend who gave his life so that Harry's dad might live.

"Let's not forget excellence, dear," added Mary Moon.

26

"What do you mean, Mom?" asked Harry, swallowing the last of his rice pilaf.

"Titus Kligore is worried about you," replied Mary Moon.

"Worried about *me*? He's a beast!" said Harry.

"He wouldn't be picking on you if he wasn't driven by fear. Don't try and punch him out in the school yard," explained Mary Moon. "Nothing good can come of that. Instead, punch him out by being great at the talent show."

"But, Mom how can Harry do that, when he's not so excellent himself?" said Honey Moon in her matter-of-fact way.

"Be quiet!" Harry shouted at Honey.

"Truth is hard," Honey added. "Let's face it, Harry Moon. You need better tricks."

Harry did not like his sister. He loved her, but he didn't like her. She was almost always right. He didn't like that either. This time, she *was* right. If he was going to beat the

bully, Titus Kligore, with "excellence," he needed
better tricks.

Harry had a good excuse to look for some superior magic tricks. When Half Moon, the family bloodhound, chewed up Harry's white fiberglass wand, Harry decided not to find a replacement wand on the Internet, but to go to an actual magic store and see if he could find a new wand for a good price. Harry had some money saved from his summer lawn-mowing business, so he peeled off a few dollars from his savings for the purchase.

Mary Moon did not much like the idea of Harry wandering around on Magic Row on his own. She thought magic was evil.

On the way home from church, Mary Moon, Honey Moon, and Harry Moon walked down Magic Row, passing by all the shop windows.

"Turn away, Harry! Turn away!" his mother would say, grabbing his and Honey's hands as they walked past the Wicca, New Age, and magic stores.

"They are just tricks, Mom," Harry replied, as he stared into the windows of the stores. "Mom, you know I like magic!"

"No, Harry Moon. It is darkness to turn young heads away from the truth."

"Want to have a look inside?" A woman with long hair and shells clanging around her neck called out to the Moon family as she opened the door to her shop.

"No thank you, witch!" replied Mary Moon. "But Mom, they're only tricks."

30

"Turn away, Harry Moon! Turn away, Honey Moon!" cried Mary Moon. "Don't you know that nothing is what it seems? Don't be so sure of those stores. They just want your money. You have better things to do than associate with that kind."

Of all the stores on Magic Row, Harry was intrigued by the shop with the most innocuous name — The Sleepy Hollow Magic Shop. It was not so much because of the shop windows, which had the latest gimmicks, but the proprietor within. He was an old, old man with big, bright eyes that twinkled even at a distance. Through the thick window glass, Harry would look at his crazy hair that stood atop his head like stacked pancakes. While the old man frightened him, Harry was also intrigued by him. He got Harry to thinking about magic.

∾

Harry Moon would lie on his bed, stare at

the ceiling, and wonder — was ALL magic an

illusion? Were all the stories, video games and movies phony? Or was magic true?

For sure, his mother didn't like magic. When Harry bought a simple magic starter kit, she tolerated it, but she did not like it. No, not one bit. But she also knew that it was his destiny.

One day, while bringing the fresh-pressed laundry into her son's room, Mary Moon noticed a poster of a life-sized man tacked to Harry Moon's bedroom wall.

"Harry, what is Tarzan doing on this newly stenciled wall?"

"That's not Tarzan."

"Sure it is, honey. I mean — look at him. He's in a loin cloth, he's half naked, and he's leaning over like an animal grunting...."

"That's Elvis Gold, Mom. He is summoning the magic. Don't you see those chains around him? He's busting them with his power."

"Power? The only TRUE POWER comes from Heaven above," said Mary Moon, shaking her head.

"Mc   at.
Elvis (is

an illusionist. He is an expert at the *Sleight of Hand*."

"How can he hide his hand? There's nowhere to put it! He is dressed like a caveman in a loin cloth!"

Mary Moon sighed as she put Harry's clean clothes in the drawers of his oak dresser.

"That's the point, Mom. He's really good. He is doing the *Sleight of Hand* without *anything* hiding the sleight. He is THAT good. He is my hero."

"Hero? Elvis Gold is your hero? The only hero you need is the good God above, Harry. Why can't you be like the other children? Horace Turner has that darling Mickey Mouse on his wall. Mark Rutherford has Abraham Lincoln in his bedroom. But *my* son? Nooo. He has Elvis Gold!"

Once Mary Moon finished, she left his room like she always did. Shaking her head. Of course,

Mary loved Harry and, likewise, Harry loved his mom. They simply frustrated one another at times.

∽

As usual, Harry was lying in bed staring at the ceiling. His lights were off and he was feeling his head for his missing hair.

There was a tiny knock on the door.

"Come in," said Harry. No one in the Moon family ever seemed to notice the "DO NOT DISTURB, THIS MEANS YOU!" sign plastered to his door.

A sliver of light entered Harry's room, illuminating his little sister in her princess pajamas, imprinted with potraits of Cinderella, Ariel, Anna and Belle.

"I was not trying to be a wise guy," Honey whispered.

"What do you mean?" Harry sighed.

"...when I told you that you need better tricks."

"What do you know? Get out and close the door behind you!"

"Mom's right, Harry. Titus is a mean boy. His sister, Clarice, is in my grade. And she is a bully just like her brother."

"What does Clarice have to do with me?"

Honey ignored the question. "Beat him, Harry. You have the magic, Harry!"

"Why are you in here?"

"I knew you were praying."

"What? Okay, maybe. But that was at least ten minutes ago!"

"I think you should do just what you were planning."

"What was I planning?"

"You were thinking of going to see that guy with that stack of hair that runs the Sleepy Hollow Magic Shop."

"How did you know I was thinking that?"

"Magic, Harry Moon." Honey smiled. "And you are a guy who needs better magic tricks."

38

THE SLEEPY HOLLOW
MAGIC SHOP

The town square was jumping that
next afternoon. It was just a few days
before Halloween. The store owners
called it *High Season* in Sleepy Hollow.

This was "Spooky Town," the scariest time
of the year, and bus loads of tourists and
consumers filled the parking lots. Everyone
was out buying their last-minute costumes
and trick-or-treat decorations for their homes.

As there was no practice that afternoon for the talent show, Harry decided to go shopping for some better magic tricks.

"Any of you guys want to come with me?" Harry asked his friends. Declan, Hao and Bailey bowed out in favor of playing Hao's new video game.

Heading to the square, Harry could not believe the line for the Headless Horseman statue. There had to be a hundred people waiting to climb the ladder and perch on the saddle for their photo opportunity. "'Tis the season," Harry muttered under his breath, shaking his head.

As Harry walked across the town green, he looked at Magic Row. Chillie Willies was very busy and so was Twilight, the shop named after the vampire books and movies. But the Sleepy Hollow Magic Shop seemed to be empty. *Maybe it's just not spooky enough*, Harry thought as he stopped and stared at it from a distance.

The shop had cheery yellow-and-red-striped awnings which shaded two windows. From far away, the awnings looked like eyelids revealing two forbidding eyes. The eyes were unblinking, staring down at Harry as he moved toward the giant face of the magic shop.

All movement of the shoppers walking through the town square faded as Harry approached the shop's unflinching eyes. As he walked slowly across the square it seemed that time itself had stopped and there was no rush to anything. The hair stood up on the back of his neck. Something unusual was about to happen. He could feel it. The wind had ceased, no sound of Slish, Slash. The square had grown silent. Only the eyes of the magic shop seemed to be awake.

Were these the eyes of the ancient Sphinx's? he wondered, "or the eyes in the pyramid on the one-dollar bill? Or are they the eyes of evil itself?"

"Dear God," Harry whispered to himself. "Please save me."

41

Harry continued in his trance toward the Sleepy Hollow Magic Shop. Crossing the square onto the street, he felt his heart start beating faster. He knew that this was his destiny.

Suddenly, a black town car came out of nowhere! It sped toward Harry as if to run him over. Harry leapt to the sidewalk in front of the shop as the car went careening by, missing him by just inches.

Harry lay crumpled on the sidewalk. He rolled over and looked off at the menacing town car as it reeled away. A bright orange sticker on the bumper flashed a toothless smile:

WE DRIVE BY NIGHT

Harry had never seen that car in the town before. *Maybe it's darkest before the dawn,* he thought to himself. "Maybe I am about to meet the dawn."

He brushed off his pants and looked toward the shop. In the eyes of the window, he saw something move! It was the old man.

The golden crown perched on his head was shining as he straightened a shelf.

Suddenly, Harry Moon found himself inside the shop. He could not remember walking through the door. He looked around. Being short for his age, he could not see much, but he could see black, rubber spiders, rubber knives smeared with plastic blood, and fly demons encased in — of all things — *ice cubes!*

43

"I have arrived!" he said with great pomp. He waited. Then he waited some more. The old man, whom he had spotted just moments before, had vanished into the bowels of the shop.

Harry's small hands clutched the lip of the counter because, truth be told, he was fearful that if he didn't hold on, his legs would collapse from under him. There was absolutely no response to his arrival — only the still air of the store. The bright slanting sun exposed a film of dust covering everything. All of it seemed so sad, so disappointingly

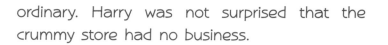

ordinary. Harry was not surprised that the crummy store had no business.

"Excuse me, sir. I am right here," Harry muscled out a voice that unfortunately did not carry the timber of a hero, but one that he was all too familiar with — his school voice. It was the voice that plagued him daily from homeroom to gym class. It was a little too thin and a little too high.

44

"There you are," someone said.

The voice was decidedly young, reminding him of Tom Paterson, his counselor from Winnapakee Canoe Camp. Harry was thrown off because he could not determine where the voice was coming from. He looked beyond the spiders and frozen flies and there, above him, floated a face that was decidedly old.

"My apologies," the man with the young voice said. "I have been meaning to put some apple boxes out front."

"Apple boxes?" Harry said, attempting to

peer over the counter. "Why would you do that?"

"So that I can look eye-to-eye with young men like you."

Harry loosened his button-down collar that seemed to be choking him.

"Man, it's hot in here," he said, coughing.

"Let me open the door. That will cool it off a bit," the old man said, walking to the door. It had a little bell attached to its spring and rang "ding-a-ling" as he swung the door open wide and, with a hook, fastened it securely to the wall so it would not blow shut.

The bracing autumn wind rushed in and filled the store with new life. Something out of the ordinary seemed to enter with it, for the room took on a wonderful magic-carpet feel. The film of dust seemed to have vanished.

Now this was the Sleepy Hollow Magic Shop of Harry's dreams — the toys and gadgets suddenly looked *slick*.

45

"I don't get that apple box thing," Harry said, finally.

"To help make you taller until you boys and girls grow into your bodies," the old man said.

"They say I am short for my age."

"Trust your Dad."

"Why?"

46

"He's right. You'll have a growth spurt soon."

"How soon?"

"When you're fifteen."

"Oh man! That's so far away!"

Turning from the door, the old man smiled at Harry. For the first time, Harry could really get a good look at the guy. He was not at all creepy like the spiders and the flies that he had for sale. But he was *old, old, old.*

"Is that better?" asked the old man with the young voice.

"So much better," Harry replied. He could actually feel the breeze on his face and knew, at least for a little while, he would not die. "Thanks!"

Although he was *old, old, old* — the man had a smile as cheery and bright as the sunny awnings that stood over the windows. His smile made Harry feel instantly welcome, not at all like a stranger. The man wore a golden crown (probably plastic, Harry thought). He was dressed in a purple cape that reached almost to the heels of his red, velvet slippers, which struck Harry as a bit inappropriate for shop attire. Those slippers would be okay for the bedroom or breakfast, Harry thought, but probably not for downtown.

"Funny you should think that," said the man. "It's all this modern footwear that keeps me from putting out the apple boxes for you."

"How's that?" Harry asked, as he followed

47

the old man back to the counter.

"The high heels of the moms. A run-in with those apple boxes could be brutal to their toes."

"Yeah," said Harry, "my dad doesn't like high heels. He says, 'Women already rule the world, so why do they have to rub it in by being taller than us guys with those *high heels?*'"

"Women like the look. I must agree with them. Their legs show off nicely in those high heels."

48

Harry squinted to really beam in on the magic shop guy. Behind his crown, Harry could see his black hair high on his head like a layer cake. Harry wasn't sure if it was a dye job or a toupee but, in the weeks ahead, he pledged he would get to the bottom of it. The old guy's eyes were the blue of periwinkle, and carried a twinkle that seemed to align with the energy of his smile.

Before he could fully take it all in, Harry was flying. He had been scooped up by the crazy old guy.

"Whaaaa?" Harry yelped, as he flew through the air, arriving on the seat of a high barstool.

"There you go," the old man said, smiling, looking at Harry, eye-to-eye. "Perfect. No apple boxes necessary!"

Harry just stared at the old man in the weird cape and crown.

49

"Now, my friend," said the old man, "it's time for the One Arm Vanish!"

"The One Arm Vanish?" Harry replied. "Hmmmm."

Harry sat on the barstool, anxious to see what the old man had up his sleeve. Every magician had a special way of using the arm as a distraction to make an object appear or disappear.

Before Harry fully knew what was happening, a cape of purple flashed before his eyes. Just as fast, it fell like a curtain from his gaze with the sunny, youthful sound of "Abracadabra!"

There in front of Harry were three different wands. Each was made of wood and varnished with a sparkling shine.

"Wow!" said Harry. "How did you know I

needed a wand?"

The old man smiled. "A wizard never shows his cards, Harry. You know that," he said. "Now, which wand is right for you? Will it be yew wood, holly wood or almond wood?"

"What do you think?" Harry said. As much as the old shop owner was sizing Harry up, Harry was sizing him up, too.

"It depends on what kind of magic you are going to practice, because there are three kinds of magic. And I would say that you haven't come here for the first kind."

"I already know table magic," Harry said. With that, the old man put aside the middle wand made of holly wood.

"Then there's the magic that comes from, as you like to say, *The Great Magician*."

"I didn't actually *say* that. I was *thinking* that. Hmmm, and I don't think I even had that thought while I was here in the store,"

Harry revealed.

"I do believe you said that in your mind while sitting here with me. Perhaps I might remind you a bit of that *Great Magician?*"

"Everyone has a little magic in them," replied Harry. "So I suppose that's the *good* magic. And then there are the Dark Arts."

"That's the third kind — the black magic."

Harry looked at the old man with the stealthiest eyes that any thirteen-year-old could ever muster. The old man's sparkle congealed into one powerful light as he stared with both eyes at little Harry Moon.

"So, Harry, what will it be — the yew wood or the almond wood?"

Harry knew that this was a test. His mother once told him that everything was a test. He looked at the beauty of both wands. Each was sturdy and each was the same length—just under a foot. "They're both the same price," said the old man. "$2.49."

Harry looked at the old man, eyes looking into eyes. On some very special level, they were connecting in a way Harry had never connected with anyone before.

"You can call me Samson. Samson Dupree," said the old man, in response to Harry's unspoken question. "And no, my strength doesn't come from my hair."

"And you can call me Harry Moon," said Harry.

"Good name," replied Samson.

"Not everyone thinks so," Harry said, as he reached out and picked up the almond wand.

Harry Moon tried to act nonchalant like an adult, but as he felt the wand in his hand, his eyes pooled up with emotion. He stared in wonder at the magical stick.

"I'll take it," Harry said.

"Why the almond one?" asked Samson.

"Yew wood comes from the Tree of Death, so that has to be for black magic. I am surprised you even sell it," said Harry.

"Oh?" said Samson, "Then answer this riddle...."

"Hit me up," Harry said more confidently, as he sat on the stool.

54

"What is the greatest gift we have?"

"Life," Harry said.

"Beyond that. What is the greatest gift in life?" Samson asked with excitement.

"The ability to choose," Harry said.
"Exactly!" said Samson.

"And why am I choosing this almond wood wand?" asked Harry.

"Because Moses led his people out of Egypt

with a staff made of almond wood."

"And how did we know the staff was almond?" asked Harry.

"Because it sprouted almond nuts from time to time. Look it up." Samson squinted at Harry. "Who's asking the questions around here, anyway?"

"We're both learning from each other. Isn't that the best way?" Harry said.

"I suppose so. Got your money?" asked Samson.

"Right here. Every cent."

"That's fine," replied Samson. "That will be $2.61 including tax."

Harry reached into the pockets of his khakis. He scrunched around. Suddenly, despite the cool breeze, Harry was feeling hot and uncomfortable again.

"I can't get to my money while I'm sitting

up here."

"Oh," said Samson, realizing. He lifted Harry up and placed him on the linoleum floor.

Harry pulled the dollars and exact change, including the tax, from his right pocket. The old man took the money, rang it up, and put it into the cash register. The register chimed with the same ring as the bell at the door.

56

"So what exactly does the wand do?" asked Harry.

"It takes you to the source of the good magic," replied Samson.

"Oh."

"Isn't that what you wanted?"
"Of course that's what I wanted. I wanted the *real* magic!"

58

Sarah Sinclair

It was at the talent show rehearsal the next day that Harry's magic started. Samson Dupree was right. There was good magic in that thing. Harry Moon had just pulled the almond wand out of his backpack. When he looked up, there she was. There was Sarah Sinclair — his former babysitter. She was a junior at Sleepy Hollow High.

When Harry picked up the wand, Sarah Sinclair came out of the shadow of the auditorium and onto the stage. She seemed giddy — as if something was about to happen — as if Harry Moon was in for a surprise.

"Sarah," exclaimed Harry, "what are you doing here?"

"I've come for rehearsal. Miss Pryor phoned me and said that, as long as I only assisted, I could help you out."

That is the best magic possible, Harry thought, practically standing on his tiptoes on the stage. That past summer, Sarah, dressed in the bangles and scarves of a genie, had been Harry's assistant in the summer magic shows he held in his backyard. Harry and Sarah had made quite a dynamic team. She was the girl in the box who Harry sawed in two. She was the keeper of the magic scarves and the top hat.

"Okay," she said, giggling, "I have a surprise for you."

Harry looked at Sarah, thinking how beautiful she was. She was running in place with excitement, her saddle shoes doing a tap dance on the stage floor. Her cheeks were flushed.

"Now close your eyes," she said. He did. "Now close them good and tight, and put your hands over your eyes."

Clamping his eyes shut and standing steady, Harry was ready. "Hit me up."

61

"I am not very good at this," Sarah said in a delightful breathlessness, "but hold on just a second, and I will be ready."

Harry could hear commotion in the background. He sensed his top hat moving off his magic table.

"Are you ready?" he asked.

"Just one more second," she replied as more noise leaked into his ears. "Okay... NOW!"

When he pulled his palms away, there was the love of his heart, Sarah Sinclair, standing in a sky-blue cardigan, holding his empty black top hat in her hands.

"Now for the fun part," she said. "Now don't laugh! I'm not good at this like you! Hocus Pocus and Razz-a-matazz and All-that-jazz!"

Her sweet incantation finished, Sarah reached into the hat and pulled out the most beauteous bunny.

He was a Harlequin, lop-eared rabbit. He was all white, except for his paws and a spotted face and ears that were as inky black as Harry's hair. The rabbit looked like he had gotten hit by a clown-pie with ink filling.

Sarah almost screamed with joy as she saw Harry's eyes go wide.

"Oh wow!" Harry exclaimed, as he reached out with the hands of a sleep walker toward the rabbit. "A real bunny!"

62

"Harry Moon!" she cried with jubilance. "Meet your new rabbit!"

"So beautiful," he whispered.

Sarah beamed her brightest smile, knowing that her gift was warmly received. She handed the huge rabbit to Harry. He clutched the rabbit to his chest and rubbed him under his chin.

"Hello rabbit. I'm going to call you 'Rabbit'," Harry said as he hugged the warm bunny. Harry gazed at Sarah with all the sweetness of his heart. "Thank you! How did you ever afford him?"

"It was nothing, really, Harry ... anything for my wonderful magician. I visited that guy at the Sleepy Hollow Magic Shop and told him I wanted to get you a rabbit for your tricks."

She smiled. "He said this was a very special rabbit and would bring you some very special magic. That's pretty cool, huh? And don't you worry, Harry. Titus Kligore has

63

"nothing on you."

Obviously, word had gotten back to Sarah about Titus bullying him.

Sarah saw that Harry was going to cry. She grabbed him and the rabbit, hugging Harry quickly as if to squeeze the tears from his eyes. They had a rehearsal to do.

"Should we use Rabbit in the show this Saturday?" Harry asked.

"Of course! Let everyone see him," Sarah replied.

"Shall we rehearse?" asked Harry.

So Harry, Sarah, and Rabbit got to work and refined the performance for Saturday night.

66

RABBIT

"Where's the new magic trick?" asked Honey Moon. She had come into Harry's bedroom to ask for some help with her algebra homework.

"Isn't Rabbit cool?" asked Harry as he rubbed the black-and-white fur of Rabbit's neck.

Rabbit and Harry were sitting on the bed.

"He's so cool that he's not even there," replied Honey Moon.

"Whaddayamean?" asked Harry, "You can't see Rabbit?"

"When I told you to get a new magic trick, I didn't mean for you to get crazy."

"Huh?" said Harry, as he looked over at the big bunny, larger than life, his face speckled in the black-and-white marks of the Harlequin.

"There's no rabbit anywhere," stated Honey Moon, as she pulled on her blond hair.

All of a sudden Rabbit spoke to Harry. "What do you want from me?" asked Rabbit. "Most people can't see me, so you have to put me into context and then they will know."

Harry looked sideways at Rabbit, surprised that he could talk.

"Context? What do you mean?" Harry asked.

"Let Honey pull me out of the hat. Context: she has to look for me in order to find me."

Harry ran over to his desk and picked his top hat up from the chair. He sat the hat on the bed. He picked up Rabbit and gently stuffed him into the hat.

Harry held the hat out and showed the inside to Honey Moon.

"Empty...right?

"Empty as your head," scoffed Honey Moon, rolling her eyes at her older brother. "I don't even know why I asked you to help me with my algebra."

"So, with one 'Abracadabra,'" said Harry, "I am going to ask you to reach inside the hat and pull out Rabbit."

"You got it," replied Honey Moon.

Harry held the top hat in his hand and took his new almond-wood wand and waved it over the black top hat.

"Abracadabra!" Harry said. "Come forward, Rabbit!"

Harry held out the top hat. "Alright, Honey. Stick your hand in the hat and pull out the rabbit."

Honey rolled her eyes a second time. With a smirk on her face, she walked over to Harry and the top hat. With her right hand, she reached in.

"Ha!" she said as her fingers flitted against the empty insides of the hat.

"Reach further!" said Harry in a commanding voice.

Honey Moon stretched her arm into the hat until it had almost disappeared. "What the heck?" she asked, feeling something. And then she screamed.

As she pulled her hand out, there was Rabbit. First his lop ears and his eyes -- and then there was more of him as she pulled him completely from the hat. In fact, Rabbit was so large that Honey had to scoop his haunches into her left hand to prop him up in her arms.

"Wow," she said. "He is heavy! What's his name?"

"Rabbit," Harry replied.

"Good name," she said. "How much does he weigh?"

"I don't know," said Harry.

Holding Rabbit in both hands, Honey Moon struggled to open the bedroom door.

Harry followed after Honey as she marched through the upstairs hallway of the house into their parents' bedroom.

Mary Moon was at the sink brushing her teeth as Honey Moon came into the bathroom and put Rabbit on the scale.

Mary looked down to see her daughter kneeling in front of the scale.

"What are you doing, Honey?" asked Mary.

"She's weighing Rabbit," Harry explained.

"I see," Mary Moon said. But, of course, at

this point she saw absolutely nothing.

"Wow!" said Honey, as the full weight of Rabbit hit the scale and the needle jumped and steadied. "Nine-and-a-half pounds!"

"That's more than I expected," admitted Harry, shaking his head.

"And why exactly are you weighing the rabbit?" asked Harry's mom.

"We need to make sure we have a big enough hat," said Honey. "He can't be breaking the top hat on Saturday night with his size. It would ruin the trick."

"Of course," replied Mary Moon as she continued to brush her teeth.

When they returned to Harry's bedroom, Honey Moon had forgotten all about her algebra, but somehow she now knew the answers.

"I have to hand it to you, Harry."

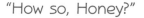

"How so, Honey?"

"When I said to get better tricks, you came through — big time."

After he said his prayers later that night, Harry climbed in his bed and Rabbit lay down at the foot of it.

As usual, Harry stared up at the ceiling before he fell off to sleep. But now, he could feel the warmth of Rabbit at his toes.

"Rabbit?"

"Yes, Harry."

"How does it all work?" the boy asked.

"How does what work?"

"You."

"Well. I'm rather like goodness... good things like kindness and gentleness and self-control."

74

"How's that?"

"Just because you can't see them doesn't mean that they don't exist."
"Uh huh."

"Remember, my human friend. The most important things in life cannot be seen."

THE WAND

There were twelve acts competing for the top prize on Scary Talent Night. As was the tradition, the show always went through a complete dress rehearsal on the Thursday night before the Saturday show. The order of the contestants was always decided by drawing numbers from a hat.

As the draw of numbers would have it, the show would begin with a bang—Titus Kligore's Maniacs were first up. The employees at Chillies had outdone themselves in building the most elaborate and authentic set and costumes for Titus and his friends. Their music was hot and dynamic. Besides all that, their coordination was good as they were athletes

Harry and Sarah sat with the other acts in the front seats of the auditorium. Her clipboard at the ready, the gorgeous Miss Pryor ran through the rehearsal with the precision of a well-tested operating system.

All Harry could think of was what his mom had to say: "Beat him with *excellence.*"

Sitting in the front row of the auditorium, watching Titus as Jason leading Freddie, the Saw, and Chainsaw Man through an athletic dance that seemed almost tribal, Harry wondered how he could ever beat these bullies with "excellence."

"Where there's a will, there's a way,"

said Rabbit.

"Huh?" said Harry. "You can read my mind?"

"For heaven's sake, Harry. There are no secrets. Besides, we should be concentrating on what *we* can do, not on what *they* can do."

"You're right, Rabbit," said Harry as he looked at the spectacular set that money and the boys' parents had put together. "It's just not fair," muttered Harry, dangling his thrift-shop top hat from his fingertips.

"Who said that life was fair? We're talking about *excellence!*" reminded Rabbit.

"Okay, okay," Harry said as he watched, mesmerized. The Maniacs even had robotic trees and fences that moved back and forth on a computer program, courtesy of Chillie Willies. When the Maniacs were finished with "Let's Get Hysterical," they sat down at the front of the auditorium with the rest of the contestants. As Titus Kligore walked down the aisle, he made sure to lay his hand on

Harry's head and made a cutting gesture with his fingers like scissor blades.

"Next time I'm gonna take it off from the neck up," Titus hissed with a laugh. Harry sighed.

The protocol for the contest was to be polite, demonstrating good sportsmanship. Anyone not adhering to the rules would be suspended from the show. Harry was not about to be a snitch, because no one liked snitches at Sleepy Hollow Middle School. Sometimes a snitch was thought to be even worse than a bully.

Through the course of the rehearsal, Titus and his Maniacs would hoot and holler when an act would finish, especially the weaker acts like Carrie Taylor with her Casper song or Tanner Douglas and his twin sisters with "Zombie Mash."

"That's enough, Titus Kligore," Miss Pryor would shout. She was not at all intimidated by Titus, even though he was a head taller than she was. She was a teacher, after all.

When Harry and Sarah stood on stage as the last act, Titus stood up before they could get a word out and shouted, "Foul!"

"Titus, sit down!" shouted Miss Pryor from the side of the stage.

"But, Miss Pryor, Sarah Sinclair is a junior," Titus answered. "She should not even BE here!"

Miss Pryor, knowing that Titus complained about everything, was prepared. With a sigh, she pulled the talent show manual from her clipboard and read from Rule 13c.

"Up to three adults can assist the participant in preparing for or exhibiting in the show on or off stage. They can *only* assist, and are forbidden from participating in the act, i.e. singing, dancing, the playing of an instrument, juggling or performing magic." She peered out over the top of the clipboard and simply said. "Sarah Sinclair is an adult, and she is assisting only. Now, sit down, Titus!"

Titus slouched down in his auditorium

chair as Sarah perked up with the mention of being an "adult". With a mature confidence previously unknown to her, Sarah twirled about the stage. She was dressed as a genie, her pink veils falling by her side.

Harry Moon's Amazing Magic Show began with the trademark tipping of his black top hat to the audience.

"So square. He looks like Mr. Do-Not-Pass-Go from the Monopoly Game," Titus whispered to Finn Johnson, his buddy.

Harry pulled scarves out of the air as Sarah delicately attached them to her costume. There were so many of them that Sarah was positively afloat with the colors.

"She looks like Cotton Candy Big Foot." Titus sneered as his pals laughed at his observation. Harry Moon's act was good, as always, but there were no new tricks—not yet.

"Can you tell me, Miss Sinclair," asked Harry, "is this hat empty?" as he showed her his top hat.

With her wrists jingling with the golden bangles around them, Sarah reached into the hat.

"Why, it IS, Mister Moon!" she exclaimed in a firm voice.

"And now I will wave my wand over the hat," said Harry in his black cape and shiny shoes. "This wand is made of almond wood—the same almond wood that, in ancient times, made frogs rain from the sky, and seas part as the people left Egypt."

"What the heck?" said Titus. "The guy is blaspheming."

"What does *blaspheming* mean?" asked his friend, Finn.

Titus and Finn watched with the rest of the competitors as Harry ran the wand over the top hat, proclaiming, "Abracadabra!"

With Sarah holding the hat, Harry reached inside and pulled out the lop ears of a black-and-white rabbit. Harry kept pulling as Sarah held the hat. As the Harlequin rabbit was slowly revealed, the rabbit seemed almost as big as Harry. The contestants broke into applause, shaking their heads. There was no possible way that a bunny that size could fit into that small top hat.

Rabbit stood on his haunches and took a bow to the audience, nodding to their applause.

"What the heck?" said Titus to Finn. "Whoever saw a rabbit make a bow like that? Must be a robot." Even Miss Pryor had a look of shock on her face, as the rabbit seemed almost anthropomorphic.

"Now," said Rabbit in a soft voice to be heard only by Harry, "take the wand and tell me to rise."

"What? This isn't in the skit," Harry whispered out of the side of his mouth, all the while smiling at his audience.

"You yourself said you have a wand that makes frogs rain. Let's get on with it."

At the risk of complete embarrassment in front of his fellow contestants, the teacher he admired most, and the junior girl in high school whom he had a wicked crush on, Harry waved his almond-wood wand over the top of the Harlequin. He commanded, "Rise, Rabbit!"

Immediately the lop ears stood up like telephone poles on either side of Rabbit's head. Rabbit's front paws stretched up toward the rafters as if he were going for a swim. Then, as the air around him took on the density of water, Rabbit began to make strokes with his front paws, and he was lifted into the atmosphere. The rabbit swam higher into the air. Sarah, with a veiled look of disbelief, opened up her arms to the audience with a smiling "discovery" stance.

The contestants in the front rows watched as the Harlequin rabbit swam above Harry and Sarah on the stage. There were no strings or wires to be seen holding up the enchantment. Rabbit then floated onto his side, and used his haunches to paddle so that he could wave like a beauty queen in a processional parade.

Sarah smiled and, through the side of her mouth, whispered to Harry, "I think it's time to bring him down."

Harry looked up at the waving Rabbit. "Return Rabbit!" he finally said, putting on a face that indicated that this was just standard procedure.

When Harry said the words, Rabbit glided lightly downward like a party balloon losing its helium. On the table stood the black top hat. With great aplomb, Rabbit fell into the opening of the hat, pouring his black-and-white fur into the funnel of the hat as if he were milk being poured into a glass.

Once Rabbit had vanished, Sarah picked up the top hat from the table and demonstrated to the contestants that the hat was now empty. With a big smile, she turned and placed the hat on Harry's head. They both bowed and left the stage.

The other contestants erupted with applause, except for Titus. His father was the owner of Chillie Willies. His father was also the mayor. If he did not win this silly middle school contest somehow, Titus would be disappointing his father. His father did not take disappointment well. Titus would have to do something about this. He clenched his fists, as did the other Maniacs, following their leader.

"Well, alright then," said Miss Pryor, obviously a little shaken by what she had just seen. "Thank you! I will see you all at 6 p.m. tomorrow night. It should be a very interesting show. Techies, please stay as I have a few notes."

Once they were at the back of the auditorium, Harry and Sarah stood quietly, trying to take it all in. Sarah's performance smile vanished.

"What just happened?" she asked Harry.

Harry looked at her. Not knowing what he was saying, yet somehow knowing that it was true, he replied, "Magic."

BAD MISCHIEF

Harry walked home alone. The wind was strong, blowing through the trees, shaking the last branches of their leaves, making the little town of Sleepy Hollow ready for a spooky Halloween. As Harry watched the dark horizon, the trees looked like walking skeletons heading to some unknown gathering of the dead.

But Harry Moon was not frightened. Even though this was the scene of Titus Kligore roughing him up the other night, he had his rabbit and his wand. He was still reeling from the real magic of the night, when Rabbit had sailed across the stage to great applause.

He took his wand out of his backpack as he walked with the invisible rabbit by his side. He turned his face upwards to the chestnut tree and waved his wand, shouting, "Abracadabra!"

Upon this command, leaves shot out of the branches and the tree bloomed. Within moments, the tree was flush with shining chestnuts. Harry blinked as the chestnuts fell from the branches, raining down on the sidewalk and yard.

He looked over at a stone wall that surrounded the Meldrum's front yard. With a simple glance at three of the stones, Harry waved his wand again, but this time over the wall, saying, "Abracadabra!"

With the incantation, the three stones

shifted into three large pumpkins which now sat on top of the wall. Harry smiled at the magic he had created. He thought a bit more and waved his wand again. The pumpkins became toothy Jack O'lanterns with big eyes. When one of the orange lanterns winked at Harry, he freaked, dashing down the road.

Harry ran so fast that he did not notice the shadowy figure in front of him. He ran right into the menacing form, falling backwards on his butt, rolling into the MacDougal's yard.

Looking up from the grass, Harry saw the large figure etched against the harvest moon. The buzz haircut and the lantern jaw could be no other—Titus Kligore!

"Give me that thing!" Titus ordered, his silhouette looming in front of Harry.

"Give you what?" asked Harry, knowing full well what he was talking about. Harry and Rabbit were both on the grass. Of course, Titus could not see Rabbit. He could only see the wand in Harry's hand.

"The wand," demanded Titus.

"It won't work for you. You're not a magician," said Harry as he clutched the almond wand to his chest.

"If it will work for you, it will work for me," insisted Titus, as he reached down to the ground. He grabbed Harry's neck in a vice grip with one hand, and with his other, he pulled the wand from Harry's grasp.

"Now let's see just who the magician is around here," said Titus. He waved the wand at Harry. "Aberkeydabya," he said, "Turn this geek to dog crap!"

Titus waited. Harry remained on the ground.

"See?" said Harry, riled up. "It isn't going to work for you."

"Oh, it will work for me, little man," he sneered. "Don't you worry."

"I'm not worried, Pharaoh!" exclaimed Harry.

"Aberkeydabyou! Take Harry to jail!" shouted Titus as he waved the wand again at the crumpled eighth grader at his feet. Titus made his command with great flare, but his gestures still did not succeed in changing Harry's locale from the MacDougal's front yard to the Sleepy Hollow Jail.

Angry, Titus took the wand into both hands and tried to break it in two like a Thanksgiving turkey wishbone.

"Sorry, dude. You are too weak. You don't have the strength to break its power," Harry said, sneering from his place in the grass. He was right. With no success, Titus threw the wand across the MacDougal's lawn. With both hands, he lifted Harry up and pushed his back against an oak tree.

Titus was massive. It was hard for Harry to hold his own.

"So what will it be tonight, Harry Moon? I guess it won't be the wand. And it certainly won't be paper. I guess it will have to be scissors."

94

Slish. Slash. Out came the sheep shears. The blades shone in the moonlight. Harry called for his wand, but it did not obey. In his mind, he commanded it in every way he could, attempting to get the wand into his hand. He was just learning its magic, and the wand did not come.

At first, Harry thought Titus was so angry that he was going to punch the scissors into his eyes. Instead, the blades rose above his eyes, and Titus took his hair. *Slish. Slash. Slish. Slash.* Off it came in clumps. Several times the tips of the scissors went into his scalp, unintentionally cutting him.

Once Titus was finished to his satisfaction, and Harry's hair was on the sidewalk, Titus looked at him and laughed.

"Why, you look like my dog Oink when he gets shaved for the summer. You are going to be happy with that, Harry Moon. Don't show yourself on stage or screen until it all grows back!"

Harry was seething, but he knew to stay quiet. By intuition, he knew there was no point in riling Titus any further until there was something he could do about it.

Titus turned and walked back into the shadows. As he moved, Harry scrambled across the lawn. He was on high alert as his eyes looked everywhere in the grass for the wand.

"Where are you, wand? Where are you?" he said, crawling through the grass. But he seemed to be alone. Harry had even forgotten about Rabbit.

There, next to the sad flowerbed of autumn where Mrs. MacDougal had raised her prize winning gardenia plants, was the wand.

As Harry reached for it, his fear gave way to a new-found courage. He called out to the shadows, "Not so fast, Kligore!" His voice was full of vengeance and anger.

The movement in the shadows stopped as Harry took hold of the wand and stood up. Never one to retreat from a dare, there was Titus Kligore, walking out of the darkness toward the small magician. "Now you'll see what real magic is all about!" Harry shouted.

"I am going to lop your head off with a cut as clean as the Horseman in the square," said Harry. "Then I am going to hide your head so you can spend your lifetime looking for it!"

"Go ahead, Magic Man! Make my day!" shouted Titus, laughing as he stood on the sidewalk, no longer in the shade of the trees, the moonlight shining on him.

Harry thrust his wand outward toward the bully. "Abracadabra!" Harry shouted, "Hide his head. May it always be misled!"

Titus waited for the magic, but nothing happened. He smirked at Harry. Undaunted, Harry tried again with more vengeful fever than before. "Hide the head—make him misled!"

"Hiding my head wouldn't mean much, little man. They say I don't have much of one to begin with." With that, Titus chuckled, shaking his head as he looked at Harry's hair. "My my, that boogie-man barber did a number on you. I suspect you won't be going anywhere for a while. Now remember, that was the boogie man, not me—or I'll come sneaking by and cut up the rest of you like you just wished on me."

With wand in hand, finished with his attempted bad mischief, Harry ran to the other side of the street, his backpack flapping on his shoulders. Titus watched as Harry disappeared into the shadows. The bully was convinced that Harry would not be back. And he certainly would not show up for the Annual Scary Talent Show!

IMAGINE

Harry noticed that only the front porch light was on as he approached his house. It was getting late. He walked to the door and looked into the foyer, but saw no one. In the glass, he caught his reflection.

"Oh no!" he cried. He saw a scared kid with chunky bits of hair sprouting from his head. Gone was the delightful, highly cultivated spilled ink bottle of hair! In its place was the fur of a road kill. Harry rustled through his backpack for his ski cap and scrunched it over his hideous head, just in case his parents were lurking about.

He snuck quietly through the front door and tiptoed across the entryway. His father was at the landing, looking down the banister.

"There you are!" shouted Harry's dad, a bright grin on his face. He was soon joined by Mary Moon, already in her nightgown and robe. "My son, the magician! The phone has been ringing off the hook!"

Hearing the commotion, Honey Moon, in her Princess pajamas, came to the banister and poked her head through the rails so she could get a good look at her brother, below. "And not just our cell phones, Harry Moon," said Honey, "but the landline as well. Whoever calls on the landline? Everyone was calling tonight!"

"Whaddayamean?" he questioned, scrunching his hat down over his hair disaster.

"Everyone's talking about your magic at rehearsal, and that you made a rabbit fly."

"Is it all that extraordinary?" Harry asked, not sure what the big deal was.

"I heard from Lila Davish," confided Honey. "Her sister is Casper in the show. She says you are a shoe-in to win tomorrow night. What did you do?"

"Knock it off, Honey!" Harry shouted. "A guy can't perform excellent magic without you making fun of it."

"Alright, alright. Come on Harry!" said John Moon, as he flopped down the stairs in his 1970's original Star Trek—The TV Show fuzzy slippers. "You and I are going to have a hot fudge sundae to celebrate."

"I'll come, too!" Honey chimed in.

"No, dear," Mary Moon said. "Your father has something to discuss with Harry."

Honey nodded as if she understood. She stoically marched back to her room in her Princess pajamas.

In the kitchen, John Moon went to work on the hot fudge sundae. *Obviously, Dad has been lying in wait for me*, thought Harry. The hot fudge was already simmering on the stove. "This must be pretty bad," Harry mused, as he slumped on the stool at the kitchen island. He pulled his ski cap deeper over his forehead.

"Aren't you hot?" John Moon asked. "Don't you want to take that hat off?"

"I feel a little chilled," replied Harry. Indeed, he was telling the truth. His road-kill head was not used to so much empty space up there on his scalp. Harry and his dad made small talk as John pulled the perfectly rounded scoops of ice cream, already prepared, from the sub-zero freezer department.

"Harry, I hope you understand that the magic you perform on stage is sheer trickery," explained John Moon. Harry could already tell that his dad's speech was as prepared as the scoops of ice cream.

"Trickery?" asked Harry.

"*Illusion*. You manipulate reality, but you're not changing it."

"Oh? Dad, have you seen my latest act? Where do you think the source of my magic comes from?" Harry asked.

"The same place the magic comes for your hero, Elvis Gold. He's very good."

"Oh, he is more than good, Dad. He is a genius."

"But, you do *understand*, Harry, that Elvis Gold is a big quack. His magic is not real." John doused the ice cream with hot fudge from the pan.

"You mean all smoke and mirrors?"

"Exactly, Harry. I know he is a great

magician. But by definition, he is a fraud. He's not really doing any of it. Let's face it. In the end, Elvis Gold is one big *phony*. That's why they call him an *illusionist*. I just want you to realize that the stuff you read in those superhero comics is just fantasy. You are not really making rabbits fly in the air. This is all pretend."

"But is it possible, Dad, to have *real* magic? After all, we live and breathe because of the Great Magician." John handed Harry the can of whipped cream. Harry was quick to spray both their sundaes with rapid-fire panache.

"There you go again, son. We call that Magician GOD. You know what Reverend Allen says about that kind of hooey."

"But it is not hooey, Dad. If the very Creator does not have a problem with my calling him the "Great Magician" when I pray, why should the Reverend?"

"Harry, you talk with too many crazy ideas. Remember, you're from the little town of Sleepy

Hollow, Massachusetts. Maybe, it's best if you don't spend all your time on the Internet. It's filling your mind with all kinds of crazy, unrealistic stuff. This is precisely the point of my talk with you tonight. Harry. You need to be more sensible about things."

"Dad, it is not the internet that is giving me such thoughts."

John placed cherries on top of the two sundaes. He slid one gorgeous sundae across the island to Harry, and kept one for himself. John Moon did not like It when his son started to talk like this. He found, too often, that Harry seemed to be twisting his words. But Harry knew his father, and he was already reading his thoughts so that he could defend himself.

"Dad, isn't my imagination part of the mind God gave me? Aren't there things to understand that can only be known through my *Spirit*, and not my eyes?"

John Moon liked it even worse when Harry

Moon talked about his *Spirit*. What did a boy know about such things?

"Look at all those miracles in the Bible," said Harry, as he took another bite of ice cream. "Wow, it's amazing Dad! People getting up out of graves, walking on water, frogs falling from the sky, sick people getting well ... all impossible things, but possible because someone believed. Did none of that happen?"

106

"Of course it did, Son."

"And weren't we told to believe? Weren't we told that we would do even more incredible things? Might that be you or might that be me? Weren't we told to become great magicians also? Or have I misunderstood what Reverend Allen has been saying all these years?"

"Well....yes...but that wasn't spoken directly about YOU!"

"Then who?"

"Don't twist words, Harry! That is dangerous!"

"All I am saying, Dad, is — if I or any of us have the gift to see what *really* is — I should be able to do some pretty awesome magic."

His father sighed. "Keep your magic pure, Harry. Don't try and do stuff that's wrong."

Harry thought about how he had attempted to separate Titus Kligore's head from the rest of him. "Okay, you're right, Dad," Harry said. He understood the wisdom his dad was sharing with him . . . with great magic comes great responsibility.

They finished their sundaes, and Harry thought, *All things considered, it went pretty well for a conversation with my dad.*

John Moon locked the front door and turned out the porch light. Together, he and Harry walked up the stairs to bed. John put his hand on Harry's back. Harry craned his neck slightly forward, afraid that John might attempt to take off his ski cap to tousle his hair. *He must know I am cold,* Harry thought. Harry was.

When Harry reached his bedroom, he dropped his backpack on the floor and ran to the mirror that hung above the chest of drawers. Harry closed his eyes, took both hands and pulled the cap from his head. Breathing deeply —as if to gird himself with strength — he opened his eyes and peered at his reflection.

"Oh wow," he whispered aloud as he stared at the boy in the mirror. What was left of his hair stood upright in patches. His scalp was a wasteland of skin and hair. He thought he looked like Briar's Field that had been hit up by Hurricane Delilah last spring.

"I want to destroy that guy," Harry muttered, fuming. He clenched his fists at the mirror and sneered. "I'm going to zing him — wand or no wand. He's the one who won't be showing up tomorrow night," he vowed. Harry sneered some more as he looked at his pitiful self in the mirror, making himself madder and madder.

"Your magic doesn't work that way," said Rabbit, peeking around from behind Harry. It didn't help that Rabbit was obviously trying to hide a very wide smile behind his very furry paws. "You have to let your anger go. The great magic is not about vengeance."

"Then what is it good for if it doesn't make me stronger than the bullies?" asked Harry, as he turned angrily from the mirror.

"Come on," said Rabbit. Opening the door, Rabbit walked onto the second floor landing. Firmly planting his ski cap on his head, Harry followed Rabbit down the staircase.

"Hi Rabbit," said Harvest Moon, as he climbed up the steps. "I love Gogurt," the toddler explained, carrying five sticks of Gogurt in his hands — strawberry, blackberry and peanut butter.

"Oh, me too," Rabbit said.

"Goodnight, Rabbit. Goodnight, Harry," said Harvest.

"He can see you? How is that? I didn't reveal you in a trick," observed Harry as they reached the entrance foyer.

"Little kids, musicians, and pregnant women—generally, they see the invisible."

Harry was always learning from Rabbit. As he walked with him, Harry grew calm.

Rabbit, his black-and-white haunches bouncing, sojourned into the kitchen. "Remember these?" Rabbit pointed to the stenciled words painted along the top of the kitchen wall. "This is what your mama stenciled with love," Rabbit said.

"I know. I have lived here for a while, remember?"

"Then you should know those words by heart, which is the intention. Read them to me, Harry."

Harry did not want to, but he knew that it would make Rabbit happy. Harry turned around in the kitchen as he read the words out loud: "Love, joy, peace, patience, kindness, goodness, faithfulness, gentleness and self-control."

Harry looked down at Rabbit. Rabbit's ink-blot face stared back at him, blinking out through his dark eyes.

"I don't see vengeance in that magic, do you?" asked Rabbit.

"No, Rabbit."

"However, I do see 'self control.' Your rabbit and your wand will serve you, Harry. You will have a magical life. It will also be a life full of trouble. We are told that. That is why there will always be times for heroes. Don't be like Titus, Harry. Be the hero you were meant to be. The world needs you," declared Rabbit.

Harry nodded, looking at the words that ran beneath the ceiling. "That's why self-control is up there."

"Exactly," said Rabbit. "You must restrain yourself so that the goodness can emerge. And it takes practice . . . lots of practice. You need to practice that as hard as you do the One Arm Vanish."

When Harry went to bed that night, he had plenty to think about. He lay awake, staring at the ceiling. In the soft glow of the full moon, his mind caught up with his soul and he slipped into a deep sleep.

Words have power. Their meaning cuts through time and space, even

dimension. As Harry floated on the words of his dream-scape — joy, peace, gentleness — he came to a great white door. He walked to the door and opened it. Walking through it, he was met with the three largest words he had ever seen. They were brighter than all the shine of New York's Time Square which Harry had seen last year when his family went to see the Christmas Spectacular at Radio City Music Hall. The words were tall. They were not a question. They were a declaration. They spoke to him, etching themselves onto Harry's soul.

113

"Yes," Harry said. "Yes. I understand. I do!"

Far away, Harry heard the chimes of the grandfather clock in the entranceway. It was midnight. As he awoke from his dream, he heard the clock chimes more clearly. In Sleepy Hollow, midnight signified the tradition of the "witching hour"—the time from midnight to one in the morning when terrible things, by legend, happened. But this was not a witching hour for Harry.

He bolted upright from his sleep as the chimes rang in his ear. He wiped his brow, covered in night sweat. He felt his head. He could not believe it! He jumped from the mattress and rushed over to the mirror above the chest of drawers.

In the half light of the new day, Harry Moon saw his reflection. His hair had grown back! There was no sign of the assault from Titus's shears. It should have been a surprise, but Harry was not all that surprised. Something had come over him ... a magic bigger than himself.

As he turned from the mirror, the shiny letters from his dream stood in the bedroom. They practically blinded him. So that he would not forget them, as he often forgot things in his dreams by the next morning, Harry wrote the words down with a Sharpie and a post-it note so he would never, ever, ever forget—the sound, the power, and the beauty of those three words . . .

DO NO EVIL

SATURDAY

W"on't you wrinkle your costume?" asked Honey Moon as she sat at the breakfast table eating her Cheerios. She was staring at her brother, Harry, who was already wearing his cape.

"Polyester doesn't wrinkle," said Harry with

an air of authority. Her brow furrowed, Honey looked more closely at Harry, scrutinizing what she could see of him rising over the table. There was writing on his T-shirt, and she just could not make it out. Harry sat beside Harvest in his booster chair. Harvest was not that hungry, given his late-night snack of five Gogurts. Still, Harry played his game of counting Cheerios with his two-year-old brother.

"One," said Harry, as he pushed the first Cheerio across the toddler's placemat. Harvest beamed as he snatched the first Cheerio, and pushed it into his mouth.

"One!" echoed Harvest after he had successfully swallowed cereal circle #1. The game continued through #2 and #3 with Harry prompting, "That's a good boy," after each. Honey found it all too tedious and boring. Honey still could not see more of the lettering beneath Harry's cape. It was hand drawn in black marker on his white T-shirt.

"Ten!" shouted Harvest as he completed his counting fun with Harry.

"Hey Superman," Honey said, "what's that say underneath your cape?"

"Oh, just a little something I put on so you could remember."

"What do I need to remember? "Honey asked with an air of indifference.

Harvest watched as Harry unclasped the button of the cape at his neck and opened his chest to Honey.

"Ta da!" said Harvest, joining in the fun. He liked it when Harry played magic with him.

"DO NO EVIL," Honey said, reading the words slowly as if for effect. "Sounds more like something you need to remember, Mr. Master of the Occult."

"That's just the point, Honey. Magic is not only a bad or a dark thing." Harry was looking around to see if his mother was within earshot. Some things were easier said when parents weren't listening. "There can be good magic, too!"

"Is that your new superhero motto, or is that your new name?" asked Honey. "You'll be big stuff after the talent show tonight. Plan on merchandising. I'm sure Dad would help set up a silkscreen sweat shop in the garage."

"No," Harry said, thinking out loud. "The phrase is more for me than for anyone else . . . to remind me of something I can't forget."

Honey was suddenly paying attention. For once, Harry was being real to her, letting her in. Honey did not want to blow her chance with her brother by giving him any 'tude in her response.

"Whaddayamean?" she asked softly.

"I just can't ever forget where my magic comes from."

"And where is that?"

"From the Great Magician."

Honey shook her head. She was back to where she started—being rather "bratty."

"Are you doing drugs? I hear everyone is doing them in middle school."

"No, I am not! And don't make fun of my magic."

"Yes, don't make fun of his magic," agreed Mary Moon as she walked into the kitchen having just walked Half Moon, the bloodhound. Harvest's face lit up with joy as he saw Rabbit enter the kitchen with his mom and his dog.

"Hey Rabbit," said Harvest.

"Hey Harvest," replied Rabbit.

"Ready for tonight?"

"Soooo ready," said Rabbit as he crossed the kitchen and headed into the entranceway.

"That's my Rabbit," said Harvest, proudly.

Mary Moon looked down at her toddler in the booster chair. His mouth was covered in milk and Cheerio smush. She picked up the side of the little one's bib and wiped his mouth clean.

"Harvest, do you have an imaginary friend?"

"No, Mommy," Harvest said. "He's right there. Don't you see him?"

"Generally, Mom, magic rabbits can only be viewed by babies, pregnant ladies, and musicians," Harry clarified.

"You mean," asked Mary Moon of her son, "highly intuitive people like musicians or innocents like infants?"

"Hmmm," Harry said, "I never thought of it that way."

"Harrumph," added Honey Moon, gulping down the rest of her tomato juice. "Apparently, Mother, Saint Harry over there has a Holy Lagomorpha which only the immature males in the Moon family converse with."

Harvest scrunched up his face in distaste and stuck out his cereal-covered tongue.

"Sorry, Harvest. But our older brother is driving us mad!"

Harry said nothing. He simply smiled and

silently pointed to the words on his chest.

"Look at that, Mother!" Honey said pointing at Harry's T-shirt. "Look at what Harry has
written on his good shirt. He ruined it!"

Mary Moon looked over from the sink where
she was rinsing the breakfast dishes. "Isn't that
nice?" Mary Moon said in reaction. "'Do No Evil.'
We should send that shirt to Congress."

At that precise moment, John Moon walked
through the door.

"Look Daddy," persisted Honey, pointing
again to Harry's shirt. "Look what Harry did to
his shirt!"

"Alright, Harry! Super cool. Kinda like the way
we wrapped up the conversation last night?"

"Huh?"

"I should remember—I rehearsed it," said
John Moon. "'At the very least, keep your
magic pure, Harry. Don't try and do stuff that's

wrong.'"

"Exactly!" said Harry, as he turned his chest to his sister, teasing her with his smile.

"Harrumph!" exclaimed Honey Moon, "This family has all gone mad. The next thing I know you will ALL be talking to the rabbit!"

"Don't knock the rabbit," Harry Moon said, "He's flying for the win tonight."

123

"What does a rabbit have to do with *excellence?*" asked Honey, fuming.

"Exactly!" said Harry, "You can't be truly excellent without being in step with the *good* magic. Rabbit helps me with all the words Mom wrote on the kitchen wall."

"Alright," said John Moon, as he went over to Harry and tousled his newly-sprouted full head of hair. "I have an idea, Buddy. I like the 'DO NO EVIL' vibe. You and I could get out the old silk screen and roll out some nice tees. Whaddaya say, Sport?"

"I say, 'Awesome', Dad!"

"What *are* you, Harry Moon, a magician or a salesman? Make up your mad mind! You are giving me a headache!" cried Honey as she jumped up from her chair and stomped her tennies against the kitchen floor.

"I'll get you an aspirin, dear," soothed Mary Moon.

124

Honey held her head high. She was bloodied but unbowed. Suddenly, she was sprayed with a batch of Cheerios. She looked over at the perpetrator. Harvest Moon, with both of his hands open, covered in Cheerio crumbs, was flicking them at her from his booster chair, incanting his own mojo on Honey.

"Abracadabra!" he shouted.

THE ONE ARM VANISH

N ews of the flying rabbit had spread
throughout Sleepy Hollow. Everyone
wanted to see the bunny fly. So by 4
p.m. Saturday afternoon, tickets sales ended
online. For the first time in its long history, The
Scary Talent Show was sold out.

A traditionally popular event, Scary
Talent was always packed, but tickets were

usually available at the door for last-minute attendees.

Not this night. This was going to be Harry Moon's night. This was the vindication of the little guy, the too-short-to-be-picked scapegoat, and the one who never got the girl. This was the high-minded desire to simply be as good as one could be. "That's what hard work and discipline can do!" said John Moon, as he rolled the last silk screen T-shirt for Harry in their garage. John was able to get such a good deal at Wal-Mart on a bulk-buy of plain-colored tees that he printed a shirt for every kid in Harry's homeroom cheering section.

Meanwhile, Titus Kligore was not worried. With his bloated sense of self, big Titus had convinced himself that Harry Moon would not be there. In fact, he was so sure that he had successfully hazed-out his competition, he convinced his dad, Maximus Kligore, to throw a victory party that night at Chillie Willies. "Anything for my winning son," said Mayor Kligore as he slapped his son's back with the great palm of his hand in admiration. "I'll get the store manager to order up the burgers and fries for the entire eighth grade. Sales at Chillie Willies have been great this year, so we'll celebrate all around. Whaddaya say, Son?"

"Sounds like a plan, Dad!" replied Titus, thrilled with the chance to impress all his classmates. But most importantly, Titus was delighted because he wanted his dad to be proud of him.

"No one," said Titus's dad, "after this party tonight, will be able to say that Maximus and Titus Kligore don't know how to throw a party!"

Something had been lost in the father-son relationship between Titus and his father. Winning had become the only thing and at all costs. It was no longer important to play fair and well.

Ring. Ring. It was the landline at the Moon household on Nightingale Lane.

"Hello?" said Harry.

"It's goodbye for you, hairy moon butt,"

127

said the rough, low voice, "if you even think about coming tonight."

While the voice was disguised, Harry knew its tongue. He had heard it in the dark. It was a voice meant to scare him by showing its power and depth. It was Titus.

Before Harry could hang up the phone, Titus hung up first. Both of them were pretty good at hanging up. They had lots of practice.

This was about the tenth time that Titus had threatened Harry that day. It was almost time to leave, and Harry was becoming worried.

He texted Sarah Sinclair to see if she could come early.

"Yes," she texted back.

An hour later, Harry, Rabbit, and Sarah sat quietly on the couch in the family room of the Moon house. The sun was already setting, the last of it slanting through the blinds. Harry closed the door.

"Oh, oh. This looks serious," observed Sarah.

"It is," Harry replied, walking over to the sofa. He took a seat between Rabbit and his ex-babysitter. Harry could not help but notice how really nice Sarah looked in her *Scheherazade* veils, bangles, and hooped earrings. Still, Sarah's natural beauty could not quell Harry's anxious heart. Nervously, he kept thumping his wand into his palm, as if to dislodge the answer as to what to do.

"What's wrong?" Sarah asked. "I see fear and courage in your eyes. Courage, after all, is not the lack of fear," she shared. "Courage is pressing forward in spite of the fear."

"Keep this on the down low," Harry said softly. "Titus Kligore has been threatening me all afternoon, making calls like a slasher right out of *Scream IV.*"

"Wow!" said Sarah. "He is really taking this Maniacs thing seriously."

"What's the solution?" asked Harry.

"You're holding it in your hand," replied Rabbit. Harry looked down at the wand in his hand.

"I can only use the wand on stage," Harry said.

"Who said that?" asked Rabbit.

"Well, when I tried to hide Titus's head . . . remember? Nothing happened."

"I believe that was more than a game of hide-the-head, Harry."

"Alright, alright. I was mad at the time."

"That's just the point," explained Rabbit. "This magic does not work from anger."

"But, I'm not angry. I'm scared."

"Then use your magic to hide yourself from your enemy."

"It can do that?"

"It can do anything that is good."

"Wow!" said Harry. "I love you, Rabbit! Where did you come from, anyway?"

Rabbit looked at Sarah.

"Well," Sarah shuffled her feet underneath

the coffee table, looking at Rabbit. "He was free. I didn't want to tell you, Harry. I thought you might think less of me, or of Rabbit. I tried to pay for Rabbit at the Sleepy Hollow Magic Shop, but that nice old man at the store refused. He said that, since Rabbit was real magic, he couldn't charge."

"Are you serious?" said Harry. "Samson Dupree charged me $2.61 for this stick!"

132

"Just a stick? I think not," said Rabbit, doing the best "tsk, tsk" sound with his bunny mouth. "Besides, you are missing the point, Harry. I come from mystery, the place where magic has its home."

"Okay, okay," said Harry as he looked at the time on the TV remote. "I am sorry, Rabbit. You really *are* priceless. I am an idiot. Can you forgive me?"

"Forgive? That's my middle name."

"It is?" said Harry, his eyes wide with performance anxiety. The show was only an hour away.

"I was only kidding," Rabbit said. "Calm down, Harry, you know your material, and we can practice the *One Arm Vanish* on the way."

Sarah stood up from the sofa, her bangles and hoops clanging against her skin. "I am so excited!" she cried. Harry looked at her and thought how absolutely gorgeous she was.

Sarah was sixteen. Her father had given her the keys to the family's blue Ford pick-up, so she could take Harry. Each of the twelve contestants had to get to the auditorium an hour early for roll call and last-minute costume and make up changes. Harry's family was going to be leaving later for the school auditorium.

Harry rode shotgun. Rabbit rode in the backseat. Sarah drove like a pro. In an attempt to not feel tiny or small, Harry sat up tall in his seat, acting casual for he had never seen his ex-babysitter drive. "Really nice on the turns, Sarah."

"Thank you, Harry," replied Sarah. "I do have one other thing to say," she added. "While he wouldn't take the money for Rabbit, the old guy at the Magic Shop did ask if he could come to the show tonight. He said he thought you should be encouraged."

"Why does he think that?" Harry asked. "I hardly know him."

"He knows more than you think he knows," Sarah said, raising her eyebrows. "I'll say only one thing more and then I will stay silent on the matter. I think Samson Dupree is your guardian angel!"

"My guardian angel?" said Harry. His eyes went glassy.

"Yes," said Sarah. "He watches over you."

"I don't even know what that means—a guardian angel. Are there such things?"

"I think there are. At least, now I do. It seems like you are his guy."

"I thought I was Rabbit's guy."

"I am from the good magic, goof. I'm not an angel," added Rabbit from the backseat.

"Stop!" said Harry. "I see him!"

"See who?" Sarah asked, looking over the wheel at the horizon.

"Titus Kligore. He and the other goons are at the curb in the parking lot, waiting for us!" Harry said nervously. "Stop the car! I have to get into *One Arm Vanish* mode!"

"Remember your magic," said Rabbit quietly.

"No, you're my magic," said Harry with a smile. Sarah slowed the car to a halt just outside the parking lot.

Without a prompt, as if he knew all along what he must do, Harry took his arm and raised it up in front of him, his cape falling in front of his eyes—a curtain hiding their bodies.

Together, entangled in the fabric of the cosmos, Harry, Sarah and Rabbit intoned in unison: "A B R A C A D A B R A !"

Waving his wand into his chest, Harry vanished under the invisibility of his cape.

To the outside world, if anyone were to look, the cab door to the pick-up truck opened, but there was no one there. While the car was still stopped in the middle of the street, the passenger door closed all by itself, or so it *appeared.*

"Hey!" said Titus Kligore, looking across the school parking lot in his convincing Freddie costume, "Isn't that Harry Moon's ex-babysitter in that Ford truck?"

"Where?" asked Finn, with a large hockey mask over his face, as he was dressed in his Jason outfit.

"There!" said Titus Kligore.

Titus and the Maniacs looked across the parking lot, filling up with incoming cars. There was no Ford truck. Titus blinked and shook his head. "I must be getting paranoid. I coulda sworn that was Harry Moon in a truck with Sarah Sinclair. Watch, guys—that Harry Moon is a sneaky one."

The invisible Harry was now riding on top of the pick-up cab as the truck turned into the parking lot, hidden from view under the folds of Harry Moon's invisible cape. Neither passersby nor Titus could see the moving car under the veil of the magic cape.

"Can you see where to drive?" Harry called out to Sarah. The cape was covering every-thing on the truck, including the windshield.

"Just fine," said Sarah, driving as slowly as the lead car in a small-town 4th of July parade. "This was NOT part of Drivers Ed, that's for sure!" she said, laughing.

Unseen, the Ford pick-up wove cautiously through the parking lot, arriving at the curb of the sidewalk which led to the front doors of the school.

With his right hand fully extended, the cloth of the cape falling from his arm, Harry slipped down the body of the truck. Crouching behind the cape so he would not be spotted, Harry walked to the driver's door and opened it. Sarah scooted herself from the seat and stepped onto the ground. She hunched down behind the cape, hiding herself from Titus and the Maniacs' view.

"Come on," Harry said to Rabbit.

Rabbit replied, laughing. "Don't worry about me. I'll meet you backstage. You got this."

"Okay," said Harry in a whisper. "Sarah, just follow my steps."

"Will do," she replied. Together, behind the cape, Harry and Sarah walked toward the school building. In front of them, waiting under the weather awning, were Titus and his Maniacs, scanning the crowd for any trace of

Harry.

Together, but hidden and frightened, Sarah and Harry proceeded carefully on their walk of invisibility to the school doors. The invisible cloth of the cape could not touch the ground — otherwise, one of the two or both of them might trip on the cloth and fall. There was just the slightest view of their feet as they walked.

Harry looked in front of him at the school entrance. He kept his focus on his destination, not on the fear he felt about the bully and his gang.

139

"Look," Titus said. "Do you see what I see?"

"What?" asked Finn.

"Look over there! Feet walking — nothing but feet walking! What the heck!" Titus shouted, pointing at the sidewalk.

As the Maniacs looked down at the sidewalk, there was nothing. Harry and Sarah had already walked past them.

"I don't see nothin'," said Finn.

Titus was unconvinced. He was sure that he had seen feet. He looked out at the parking lot and he saw what he thought he had seen before.

"I'm not going crazy, guys," he said. "I just saw feet, and I *know* I saw Sarah Sinclair's truck before 'cuz there it is!" He pointed again and, this time, at the end of his finger, was Sarah Sinclair's blue truck parked at the curb. He ran to it and the Maniacs ran, too, — not knowing what else to do.

"I knew it! I knew it!" Titus shouted, clutching the handle on the door of the truck. "Those sneaky ones are here!"

"What do you mean — they are here?" asked the guy dressed as Werewolf. "How could they have gotten here?"

"Magic," Titus said. "*Real* magic."

140

"Wicked magic?" asked Finn.

"I don't know. I can't be sure," said Titus, as he turned away from the truck door.

Even though all the Maniacs were in masks or clay make-up, their eyes betrayed the fear that was in their hearts. They were wondering — who was this Harry Moon character and what type of magic was he playing with?

"Come on, guys, we are letting our competitors get the best of us, " said Titus. "There is no such thing as *real* magic. It's all tables and chairs. Now, let's go WIN this dang thing."

141

Meanwhile, Harry, Sarah and Rabbit were already backstage, getting ready for the performance that would change their lives forever.

142

THE
SCARY TALENT SHOW

"Miss Pryor, I don't mean to be a snitch, but I do not believe that Harry Moon is competing in good sportsmanship," growled Titus. He towered over the Drama and Arts teacher, cornering her in the hallway.

"Why do you say that?" said Miss Pryor with a sigh. She knew Titus's tactics too well.

The Kligore family was accustomed to getting its way.

"I think that Sarah Sinclair is doing more than assisting. That's against the rules," complained Titus.

"I have seen nothing in their show that would justify your accusation, " the teacher said, with a huff.

"And what about that stupid rabbit? That's no rabbit. He's a beast. Did you see the size of that thing? Some kind of monster. Keep an eye on that *thing*," he said. "You wait for it, Miss Pryor. It's the rabbit that's running the show. Harry is assisting. It's not even Harry doing it — it's some kind of black magic. My father, the mayor, supports the ideal of Spooky Town, but not spooky magic — not *black* magic!"

"Thank you, Titus. I am sure our judges will be watching carefully."

Pushing her bangs off her forehead, Miss Pryor, with her clip-board firmly at her side, walked backstage to the stage manager, asking if Harry Moon had signed in. He showed her his own clipboard, revealing Harry Moon's signature on the line at 6:20 p.m. "He's here somewhere. I have not seen him since he signed in on the board."

Miss Pryor played by the rules. She did not particularly like Titus Kligore's oppressive personality, but something that Titus had said was rattling her.

The show began promptly at seven o'clock. Miss Pryor stepped into the spotlight on the stage and announced the eighth annual Scary Talent Show. Miss Pryor was high energy — her smile gleamed to the packed audience. There were even people sitting on the aisle steps in the balcony watching. Miss Pryor began the evening by congratulating the many "wonderful" acts from "many of our talented students."

The Maniacs were on board first. They all

came onto a stage replete with tall, wintry trees. The group appeared behind a cloud of dry ice, courtesy of Chillie Willies' event planners.

Titus had a strong baritone voice. Despite his unfair tactics, Titus was a terrific singer. The Maniacs sang the hit song, "Let's Get Hysterical", with acappella skill.

As the Maniacs' song continued, their costumes were transformed before the eyes of the audience. At the crescendo of the song, the singing group all became wolves. The technical brilliance of the act could not be denied. As the Maniacs hunched down onto the floor, a massive orb of moon fell from the rafters, suspended in the air. Black crows from the skeleton trees took flight, cutting silhouettes across the moon while the Maniacs all howled.

Harry, Rabbit and Sarah watched from stage left. Harry studied the Maniacs' act. "They added that cloud of ice and the crows since dress rehearsal."

Sarah nodded. "Yeah. I guess it helps when

your dad owns the biggest store in Sleepy Hollow," she said.

"He has a bunch of money to do fancy stuff like that," said Harry. He pulled the backstage curtain enough to be able to look out at the audience. He was surprised. They gave the Maniacs thunderous applause, but no standing ovation.

"We gotta play fair," said Sarah.

"I know," said Harry, turning away from the curtain. He looked up at his ex-babysitter. She was so beautiful. "Besides," he said to himself, "she is nice, and smells good."

"Thank you, Sarah, for helping me out," Harry said.

"No problemo," Sarah said, smiling.

"I hope someday, you will see me not as a guy you used to babysit but just a guy," he said.

147

"I do, Harry. I already do," she said sweetly.

"That's a nice crown you are wearing," Harry said.

"Oh, thanks! Do you like it?" she asked. "I added it at the last minute. It's actually called a 'diadem', and it has a little veil. I got the idea from *I Dream of Jeannie.*"

148

Harry was beside himself. "*Wow!*" he thought. *Listen to her. She already sees me as a guy! I am making progress, and she hasn't even gotten my Christmas present.*

"I wouldn't be here if I didn't care about you. But you know, Harry, there will always be the age difference between us."

Yessirree, Harry thought, gobsmacked. *I am making real progress.*

∾

While the other acts took the stage and

performed, Titus lurked backstage, hunting down Harry and Sarah. There were no clues. No one had seen them. Of course, Harry and Sarah were wrapped in the magic of the cape.

Harry's heart knocked against his ribcage as Miss Pryor walked onto the stage to introduce the final act. Harry looked out at the judges' table next to the orchestra pit. The three judges were engaged, still fresh. "Being last can cut both ways," Harry thought.

As Harry took the invisible cloak away, revealing both himself and Sarah, the stage manager came up to them. "There you guys are!" the manager said. "I gotta get your mics on." With rapid-fire efficiency, he put the wireless mics on both Harry and Sarah.

"Ladies and gentlemen! I am pleased to present Sleepy Hollow's final act of the evening — The Amazing Adventures of Harry Moon — starring eighth-grader, Harry Moon, assisted by Sarah Sinclair."

Harry put on his top hat. He turned to

Sarah, who adjusted it on his head.

"Go get 'em, Moon Man," she said, smiling.

Harry looked into her soft blue eyes. He thought he would fall in. "I believe in you," they blinked back.

"This was it!" he thought. "She's going to kiss me on my lips." Alas, not yet — but a thoughtful kiss on the cheek was more than enough for the moment.

Harry smiled at Sarah, and with a wink, took a deep breath and turned to meet his audience.

To a sparse splattering of applause, Harry marched onto center stage. He looked like a cartoon character. His black velvet top hat was too big for his short, sparkplug body.

Beneath the single spotlight he stood — a lonesome, solitary figure — quite the contrast to Titus's loud and boisterous group.

"Good evening, ladies and gentlemen," Harry

said. He stood quietly, waiting for the silence to collect itself. Then he stood there even longer. Someone coughed in the auditorium, and the sound thundered in the hush.

In the thirty-fifth row on the first level of the auditorium, Mary Moon grabbed her husband's hand.

"Dear God, our boy has stage fright!" Mary whispered through clenched teeth.

"Come on, Sport," said John Moon, encouraging his son. Harry Moon looked out at the packed crowd. His eyes swept the audience. He saw his family. He saw Samson Dupree. He saw the ten rows of Kligores.

Honey Moon looked at her brother, the blood draining from her face. "I knew this would happen," she proclaimed to her parents in a whisper." He's choking up out there! I won't live this down. I am ruined."

Harvest Moon sat in Honey's lap and reached up with his tiny hand and put his

gooey fingers into her mouth. He wasn't playing with her tongue — he was silencing it.

But Harry wasn't choking up. He was
seizing his moment, making sure that the
audience was completely with him. All eyes —
including the eyes of one Titus Kligore — were
on the stage, waiting, hushed, riveted in the
silence, to see what this young magic man
would do. "I just knew it." Titus said, seething to
Finn and Freddie, "I told you he was a sneaky
one. Lookit! He even got himself a wig."

Harry smiled. And in that instant, the
audience became Harry's personal plaything.
The crowd let out a collective sigh, assured
that this funny-looking performer with the top
hat knew exactly what he was doing. Harry
was running the show from his small circle of
spotlight. Harry Moon had learned well by
studying the master, Elvis Gold.

"It's strange being here, don't you think?" he
asked the crowd as he walked across the stage.
"The mystery never leaves us."

Mary Moon shuddered, "Oh no." Her grasp on her husband's hand went tighter. "What is he doing?"

"I'm not quite sure, sweetheart," said John, the effervescent encourager of his son.

"I'm not speaking of this stage," said Harry, addressing the audience. "I am speaking of life."

"It's strange, being visitors in this world. As hard as we try, we don't quite get it. We see glimpses of something more — a deeper magic. I see it in my little brother's eyes. I see it in the beauty of the sunrise."

Harry extended his arms wide open to the audience. "But, as hard as any of us try, we don't ever have all the answers. So tonight, please sit back and relax, as I hope to take you through a doorway into the wonder that lies behind that sunrise. Sarah Sinclair, if you will assist me?"

With her genie scarves trailing her,

Sarah walked onto the stage, finding it difficult to hide her smile. She was infatuated with this young magician. Sarah had no idea what was about to happen, but she didn't care. Whatever Harry Moon was selling, she was buying.

Sarah was a very graceful assistant. She was a junior in High School, after all. She was liked by most of the girls in middle school. They looked up to her and she had a good eye for fashion, too. They liked her outfit, especially her diadem with the veil.

Harry had silenced everyone. This was the show they had come for.

Sarah smiled reassuringly as she reached Harry. Harry tipped his hat knowingly to her and took her hand to introduce her to the audience. Sarah tipped her diadem to him. It was a lovely sign of respect. The audience clapped in appreciation.

"How adorable," Mary Moon said.

"If you like kitties with bows and unicorns," Honey Moon said, scornfully.

"What does THAT mean?" asked John Moon.

"Cheese ball," answered Honey Moon, scrunching herself down into her seat.

Harry handed his top hat to Sarah. She held it, walking to the rim of the stage, revealing the emptiness inside of the hat to the audience members and to the judges.

When she returned to him, Harry opened his palm.

"Abracadabra!" he commanded.

Harry turned his palm in the sleight of hand. He turned it back to the audience and there, in the grasp of his fingers, was the almond-wood wand! With Sarah at his side, Harry placed the wand above and below the hat, running it through the empty spaces to show the audience there were no wires or

hidden cabinet supporting the hat.

With a grand gesture, Harry waved the wand over the hat, saying, "Abracadabra!"

Mayor Maximus Kligore looked on from the third row behind the orchestra. He squinted his eyes, watching carefully. He had brought his bird-watching binoculars along, just in case Moon made it to the stage. He was studying the magician's every move. He would expose the fraud, and save the trophy for his son.

"That's odd," muttered Maximus to his assistant, Cherry Tomato, from behind the binoculars. "That wand he is using is not made of yew wood."

"How can you tell that from here?" Cherry asked. She had the most unusual eyes — cat-like. "What is it, then?"

"I have never seen one before. It's almond wood."

"So?"

"Almond wood. That's the same wood, so the story goes, that was used in Moses' staff for all those miracles. Remember the Charlton Heston movie?"

Cherry Tomato sat up with a bolt, as if she had just been given a shot with a very long needle. She grimaced — a look that suggested she did not like what her boss said. No, not one bit.

Meanwhile onstage, Harry reached his hand into the top hat. The audience drew in its collective breath. They had heard stories about this young one. No one knew what to expect.

157

Harry's arm fumbled around inside the hat, stretching, until he hit on something. His body stiffened. As he yanked, the hat yanked back. The smile on Harry's face froze. His arm disappeared down into the hat. Harry was lifted into the air by the pull of the magic. With Sarah struggling to hold the top hat firm, Harry's head, shoulders and chest were pulled into and vanished inside the top hat.

Slish. Slash, went his legs, wig-wagging back and forth in the air, upside down out of the hat. The crowd gasped. In the middle of the spotlight stood Sarah — all alone — her face straining, gallantly fighting to hold the wiggling hat upright, half of Harry in-side it, his legs swimming in space. No one could be *that* strong to hold that hat upright for very long.

The audience rose to its feet in a mixture of fear and awe. Women screamed.

"That's the occult! John Moon — we are witnessing our son going straight to hell!" cried Mary Moon.

"What if that's not hell, Mary?" yelled John Moon over the crowd's shrieks.

"What else could it be?" she shouted back. She was on her feet, rushing down the aisle towards the stage to save her son.

Mary knew Sarah Sinclair well. She was too stressed to read the expression on Sarah's face. If she had, she would have seen Sarah shaking

her head ever so slightly at her. Mary stopped and stood near the stage.

Sarah turned the hat over to the side, holding it firmly between her arms. Harry's scissoring legs flipped sideways with the hat. She turned the hat toward the audience, with the real-live kicking boy inside it.

Sarah then flipped the hat over and Harry's feet hit the floor. As they did, he let out a big "Ah ha!"

159

His feet — and only his feet — were on solid ground.

Never had there been anything like this before in the Sleepy Hollow Middle School. Harry was running around the stage like a mad *Road Runner* cartoon with just his legs and feet sticking out of the hat. There was no sign of the rest of him.

"Ladies and gentlemen! May I introduce Sleepy Hollow's very own Headless Magician!" proclaimed Sarah.

The audience did not know whether to applaud or call the Fire Department. They were on their feet screaming. The hat stopped running — the spotlight running to it.

The hat took a bow.

Transfixed, the audience watched as the legs buckled to the floor and Harry's body wrestled inside the hat.

Mimicking the sounds of the thousands of hours of cartoons he had watched as a kid, Harry created a pandemonium of fighting noises inside the top hat. With the speaker system at full tilt, the theatre reverberated with the imagination of his soul.

"Rugrats!" yelled Harvest Moon, jumping up and down on his sister's lap. "Harry KNOWS that's my favorite show!"

"Big deal," replied Honey Moon.

As Harry wrestled on the floor, he leveraged himself with the hat, attempting with great determination to free himself. First, his chest popped out and then his shoulders. Finally, his head and his arms appeared.

The spotlight burned hot as Harry lay exhausted and sweaty on the floor, fully revealed except for his hands. Rolling his back against the floor boards, Harry struggled upward until he was standing upright, his hands still inside the hat.

With her scarves flowing, Sarah approached the hat. With the precision of a registered nurse, she began to pull on it from the other side. As she did, Harry's hands were exposed, holding what looked like a huge white snowball. But as Sarah pulled further, it was not a snowball at all. It was white fur . . . and then more white fur . . . and then black fur . . . and then grey and black-and-white fur. There, like a banner unfurling, was the largest lop-eared Harlequin rabbit anyone had ever seen!

In the audience, Samson Dupree, his hair pomaded flat so that people behind him could see, leaned over to a set of five-year-old twins and said, "Wow! That was some hat trick, don't you think?"

162

"Epic!" said the twins in unison.

Samson turned to the twins' father and handed him his Sleepy Hollow Magic Shop card. "Come by the store sometime if you want a rabbit all your own. I don't take cash or credit cards. The rabbits are free."

"Oh, I don't know," said the father.

"No rabbit pen necessary. No upkeep. You just gotta show love and respect to a little rabbit. "

"Yes!" cried the twins, in unison once again. Yet it was not in response to anything Samson Dupree said. It was what they were watching on the stage.

Rabbit was standing quietly before the audience. His black-and-white face, like a clown mask shining from beneath the spot-light, smiled as he took a bow.

"What?" Harry said, as if Rabbit were talking. "You don't want to go back into the hat?"

163

Rabbit shook his head, "No."

"Then where will you go?" asked Sarah, listening as if the rabbit were talking.

"You want to go flying?" asked Harry.

Rabbit nodded his head, "Yes!"

The audience stood in silence. This is what they had heard about. They had come to see the rabbit fly. They did not want to miss

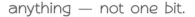

anything — not one bit.

"You are going to fly like the wind?" Sarah asked.

Rabbit nodded his head.

"You want to blow wherever you please so we will hear your sound, but we won't know from where you come or from where you are going?" Harry asked,

164

Rabbit nodded excitedly.

Harry walked over to Rabbit. He picked up his top hat and put it back on his head. There was even a bit of a swagger in Harry's saunter.

"Then you know what we have to say about that, Sarah?"

"Oh, I do," she replied with a smile.

"It's really quite simple . . . a simple word — Abracadabra."

"Can the audience say it with us?" Harry said, raising his voice.

"Yes!" many said.

"Good," Harry replied. "Then -- on the count of three. One. Two. Three!"

"A B R A C A D A B R A!" the audience yelled.

"What is this, a rock concert?" asked Honey Moon. Harvest Moon laughed, putting his fingers in her mouth again.

The people in the audience lifted their eyes as Rabbit rose silently from the stage. Like an untethered helium balloon, Rabbit floated gently, effortlessly. Once he reached the top of the proscenium, he turned his bunny face to the audience.

He sailed — not swam — across the ceiling. This time he did not paddle with his haunches or paws.

The houselights were turned down low for the show on stage. There was no need to turn them up now for everyone could see the sailing rabbit. They watched Rabbit, but everyone would tell you later they were watching something other than a rabbit. They were a witness to real magic.

The fur of Rabbit expanded as he sailed, growing into a great silver cloud. At the top of his flight — as Rabbit fell from the ceiling above the audience — he broke apart into snowy particles. The auditorium was filled with the gentle flurry.

Mary Moon was struck by the beauty as she watched the silver fur fall. Standing next to the stage she realized her son did not need to be saved after all. No longer stressed, she returned to her seat with her family.

As Rabbit fell like snow flurries, the audience's eyes were redirected by the spinning trajectory of the snowflakes back toward the stage. It was snowing everywhere, even on stage upon Harry and Sarah. It was silent. Like a first snow on

warm soil, it did not stick. This snowfall simply vanished into thin air.

"Thank you, everyone!" said Harry. "May the magic never leave you!"

Sarah came up behind him. She unclasped his cape and dropped it from his shoulders. And there it was.

"Hey, those letters turned out well, don't you think?" said John Moon to Mary.

167

"They look great, John," Mary replied, still a bit dazed.

On the stage, Harry was wearing one of the tees that he and his dad had silk screened that afternoon.

DO NO EVIL

What happened next that night is still spoken about today in Sleepy Hollow. When Sarah dropped the cape from Harry's shoulders, the amazed audience stood in silence, taking in the young magician, his assistant, and the magic that had filled the auditorium.

Someone from the third row (they say it was one of Titus's gang) was the first. With a shout of "Bravo!" he started to clap furiously. The theatre was filled with shouts of appreciation and thunderous applause, which seemed to go on forever. Harry had given them the show they had come for.

"Do no evil" was what they wanted to do, after all. Even though it was sometimes hard, people wanted to do good. As Harry Moon said, "There is deep magic in all of us."

Mayor Maximus Kligore sneered as he turned to his assistant, Cherry. "Do no evil? We will just see about that." He punched a text message into his phone and pressed send.

At the judges' table, a phone vibrated with a text alert. A Sleepy Hollow Selectman glanced at the message and sighed. This evening was about to get ugly.

LOSS

Titus and his Maniacs won the Scary Talent Show. Before she announced the winner, Miss Pryor announced that the Amazing Adventure of Harry Moon act had been disqualified. She was expecting the moans

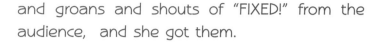

and groans and shouts of "FIXED!" from the audience, and she got them.

"The judges have ruled that under Rule 4, Section G, the performance is disqualified because of a co-performer who was not on the Middle School roster," she explained.

"Sarah Sinclair only assisted," shouted John Moon, standing at his seat.

"It is not because of Sarah Sinclair, John," said Miss Pryor. "It was because of the ... er .... the exceptional rabbit. The judges believed that the rabbit was not, for lack of a better expression — *a prop* — but rather the rabbit co-performed with Harry Moon, executing stunts that would be reserved for a performer, not a prop. And Rabbit is not registered in Middle School."

When Titus and the Maniacs were declared the winners, there were a lot of haters including almost everyone in the eighth grade. The biggest haters of all were Harry Moon's friends — Hao, Bailey and Declan. "I'm gonna punch that guy at his own party!" said Bailey, really angry. "Who's with me?"

Declan and Hao said they were with him, but they suggested they just scare Titus instead. Once he calmed down, Bailey agreed. They knew Chillie Willies fairly well. They would entrap Titus Kligore in the "Haunted Cube" of the shop, and run scary moments from the top 100 scariest movies of all time and drive him mad.

"Hey, guys, I appreciate your sentiments, but just let it go, okay?" advised Harry.

"We'll see," said Bailey, which was code for "No".

They were standing outside the covered sidewalk of the middle school. The parking lot was humming with people leaving.

"Great show! Fantastic, Harry! Bummer on the ruling. You should have won!" came the shouts to Harry from everywhere. Many simply came up and interrupted the guys in order to pat Harry Moon on the back or to just shake his hand.

These interruptions were fine for Declan, Bailey, and Hao. It was easier to bear their discomfort with Harry's attractive ex-babysitter standing right next to them.

"Are you going to the weasel's party?" asked Declan of Harry.

"I think I should show, don't you?"

"I think that's the right thing to do," Sarah said. "Good sportsmanship and all."

"Good sportsmanship? From whom? Not that scum of a bully! 'Fire with fire' I say!" exclaimed Bailey.

"It just shows who is the bigger man," said Harry. "That's all."

"Bigger man?" said Declan. "You lost, Buddy. That's how it will read Monday in the school paper."

"I won! I had the good magic," Harry replied.

"Really? Where's your trophy? Oh? You don't have it? That's because you were robbed of it!"

The Selectman from the judges' table came up to the group. "Your show was spectacular, young man," he said, as he reached out and shook Harry's hand. "I'm sorry that the rules could not allow for the appropriate public acknowledgment."

"Thank you, sir," Harry said, putting on a smile.

The Selectman backed away from the others and walked to a black town car. The other judges were waiting for him. They were happy and talkative, pouring themselves into the car.

"Look at them," said Hao. "A bunch of sad hypocrites. Look at that! What the heck is that on the bumper? *We Drive By Night*? Have they read too many Twilight novels or something? What are they? Vampires?"

Harry winced at the sight of the *We Drive By Night* bumper. That was also on the bumper of the car that almost ran him down when he visited Samson Dupree at the Sleepy Hollow Magic Shop.

"I am telling you all right now. This town is not what it seems," said Bailey. "It is not some quaint little 'Spooky Town' selling quaint spooky trinkets and Headless Horsemen dolls to tourists. This town is the real deal. It is evil to its core. One minute, the town is in bankruptcy -- the next minute, the Selectmen are driving around in limousines! So, are you coming with us, Harry?"

"I can drive you, if you would like," Sarah told Harry. "The truck is right over there."

"You have a truck?" said Hao, impressed and trying not to show it.

"It's my dad's."

"Hey, thanks Sarah, but no thanks," replied Harry.

"Better that you're not implicated as an accessory to the crime."

"I'm not your getaway driver," Sarah said.

Hao, Bailey, and Declan started to walk away to the party. They were so not able to understand girls.

"You coming, Harry?" said Bailey, turning around.

"Ah .... er...," Harry said, confused, turning to Sarah. "I gotta figure out what ...."

"Oh," said Bailey, "We get it. You gotta figure out about the truck."

"Something like that," said Harry.

Once the guys were gone and most of the cars had left, Harry sat down on the stone bench on the covered sidewalk and started to cry.

"I'm sorry," he said, as Sarah sat down beside him. He tried to hide his face with his arm. But he was tired, and not really wanting to do a *One Arm Vanish*. "I didn't want you to see me like this."

Sarah slipped the veil off her costume, bunched it up and handed it to Harry for a much-needed handkerchief. "That's okay. I've seen it before," Sarah said. "After all, I was your babysitter."

"Oh, yeah. Right!" Harry said, remembering,

as he blew his nose into the pink veil. He looked up at her with his wet eyes. "But you don't see me that way anymore, right?"

"Right," she answered.

"So maybe time will change things, right?" he asked.

"Time will change all of us. But I will always be a girl who is three years older than the boy. Think of it! When you are a freshman next year, I'll be a senior. I'm afraid that this just cannot be."

"Don't say that, Sarah! I don't like it when you talk that way."

"This girl has always talked that way, Harry — ever since I stopped babysitting you. I have never misled you... have I, Harry?"

"I guess not," he answered as he blew into the veil again.

Rabbit appeared and sat between the two

of them on the bench. He put one paw around Harry and his other paw around Sarah.

"I simply want to get this on record," Rabbit said gently, but with enthusiasm. "As far as love is concerned, both of you need to promise me ... because many, many people will try to separate me from you ... promise me that you won't ever leave me!"

"If you promise us that you will never desert us," Harry replied.

"Never, ever *ever!*" said Rabbit.

"Then it's a deal," Harry said.

"Deal?" asked Rabbit of Sarah.

"Deal," she replied.

"I'm sorry about tonight," Rabbit said. "But the world is not fair. That's why it needs heroes. It probably won't get any easier. Sarah ... Harry. I am going to break it to you gently — having a friend like me has its consequences."

THE HAUNTED CUBE

B y the time Sarah and Harry pulled
up in the Ford pick-up, Chillie Willies
was jumping. The neon signs were
flashing "Congratulations, Maniacs!" The
winning gold trophy was in the center of the main
showroom. Titus Kligore and his Maniacs stood

by the trophy for the photo ops. Within minutes, *Instagram* was flooded with Maniacs shots. It looked like the entire eighth grade – about 200 in total — had shown up for the party.

Meanwhile, Declan and Bailey had a trust-worthy reputation with their classmates for being trustworthy. By telling Harry's story, they were able to stir up a deep sense of injustice in the hearts of their friends. Most of them had also experienced being bullied by Titus. It was easy to stir up the hate. There were at least three dozen girls and boys working together to scare Titus out of his senses. "Not that he had much sense to begin with," observed Hao.

In fact, they had so many students in on the gag, they had already rigged the "Haunted Cube" of Chillie Willies to accommodate vengeance against Titus. The Cube was a hot ticket in the showroom, especially popular with high school seniors looking for a good time at graduation. It also involved a test of will. It was a virtual haunted house walled with forty LED screens that showed scary stuff. You were essentially locked in the cube until you screamed.

Then, you were taken out of it.

The record for the longest time in the cube was held by Adele Cracken at three minutes and twelve seconds. Adele had had the flu and could neither see nor hear at the time, so many called "foul," but she remained the winner of record.

The PTA tried to shut down the "Haunted Cube" for years, calling it a *nightmare provoker,* but Maximus Kligore always won out with his "good clean scary fun" pitch.

Clooney Mackay, a super-brilliant techie, split the data that ran into each existing screen into four quadrants. What this meant was that in the haunted room, there would not be 40 scary movies playing at once, but 160. "Heck," said Clooney, his eyes bouncing with electric excitement. "Even the Dalai Lama would go bonkers from this."

"This won't kill Titus, will it?" asked Bailey. "I promised Harry we would just mess him up."

"Of course it won't kill him," Clooney said, laughing in anticipation. "But this will be a Halloween he will never forget!"

While kids danced and ate, something else was going on at the party. Everyone was texting their own nasty photos and videos of Titus to Clooney's cell phone. The cell fed into his computer. "All the nastiness is from him," said Clooney to his girlfriend, PJ McDonald. "It's about time he got a whiff of his stinky self."

182

"This is pure evil," complained PJ as she parked both hands on her hips and huffed. She was standing by Clooney's laptop at the back of the "Haunted Cube" while several of their classmates were rigging the guts of the LED screens with the feed cable.

"It is not evil, PJ! An eye-for-an-eye, right?" Clooney said.

"You obviously did not read far enough," PJ replied. "It's 'turn the other cheek'."

"Fine. We'll turn his cheek once he gives us

an eye!"

"Fools! All of you!" PJ said, looking at her friends, now puffing in exasperation. As she walked away from Clooney, she tossed her chestnut hair to accentuate her disapproval. Several of the students flattered Maximus Kligore in the party- favor section of the store.

"Where did Titus get that voice, Mister Kligore? It is so awesome! It must have come from you."

"Well I did sing in the choir until my voice changed," Maximus said with pride.

Meanwhile in the costume showroom, Larry "the Locksmith" Loneghan was busy behind the door of the "Haunted Cube." Since his dad ran the Loneghan Hardware Store, Larry spent a lot of growing-up time making extra keys for customers. Larry became an expert on locks. He found a way to override the safety system in the Cube that ensured no one could get locked in it and go insane.

"As Mr. Kligore would say, this is just 'good clean scary fun', right?" Larry said to Hao, who was looking over his rigging.

"That's one way of putting it, Larry," said Hao.

So many people were busy scheming that no one noticed Harry, in his cape, and Sarah, in her Scheherazade silkies, entering the front door of Chillie Willies.

"Are you sure you are okay with this?" replied Harry, looking up at the beautiful Sarah. He practically had to shout as the music was really loud.

"Why wouldn't I be?" shouted Sarah.

"It's eighth grade." He shrugged his caped shoulders

"So?" she said with a smile. "It's nothing to be embarrassed about. We all go through eighth grade at some point."

"Let's hit the snack table," he suggested.

"I'm with that," she agreed, following Harry through the crowd. The music was loud, the dancing was fast — but something else was at work. Harry sensed something in his soul. His intuition kicked in. There was tension in the air. No one was talking, as if waiting for something to happen.

"What would you like?" Sarah asked, as she arrived at the snack table. It was loaded with every kind of candy. And there were popcorn balls.

"Oh thanks ... a Coke," said Harry, distracted. He saw Hao trying to hide a suspicious expression in his eyes.

"What's going on, Hao?" Harry asked.

"We're just waiting for the scream."

"What scream?" Harry asked.

"The scream that comes from the big fat

mouth of Titus Kligore once he gets his fill of every terrible thing he ever did to any of us plus *Scream 1, II, III, IV,* and *V*," Hao said, eating a Hershey's Kiss striped in Halloween orange and black.

"Where is he?" Harry asked.

"In the Cube."

"In the Cube? I warned you guys," Harry said.

"Hey, did you hear him?" asked Hao.

"How can anyone hear anything with the music so loud?" Harry shouted.

"We had to turn it up so old man Kligore wouldn't stop us. We have him in the party-favor room telling tales to his adoring fans," Hao said with a smirk. "Hey, did you hear it that time?"

"Hear what? The Cube only allows for one scream," Harry said.

Sarah walked over with the Cokes and handed one to Harry.

"What's that screaming?"

"You hear it?" said Hao.

"I have sensitive ears, "Sarah explained. "Is it a new ride or something?" she asked. "There's an awful lot of screaming!"

Hao laughed. "That's because Larry the Locksmith overrode the security door. Fat-mouth Titus is not getting out from that slammer of horror any time soon."

"Whaddayamean?" asked Harry.

"He robbed you of your glory, Harry. We don't like that. He and his dad have this town trick-wired for their own pleasure."

"He was good tonight. All the Maniacs were!" Harry responded.

"Yeah. But you, Sarah, and Rabbit blew it

up! Hey! Where is Rabbit, anyway? Is he coming by for a Coke, or is he still in the atmosphere?"

Not even the music could mask the now constant screaming. Harry looked across the makeshift dance floor and the sea of dancers. He could see that the Cube was not only rattling — it was rocking from side to side.

It was rumbling with such crazy energy that all the kids had moved away from it.

188

Then it happened. There was a low sounding explosion when the Cube erupted in flames. It was Halloween after all. It took but an instant before the fire licked up the wall of Halloween costumes. Highly flammable, the costumes fired up in vivid orange and yellow. The flames hit the net on the ceiling, loaded with scary stuff. As the flames from the Cube tore at the nylon netting, skeletons, plastic gravestones, spiders, bats, and stuffed zombies fell onto the dancers.

Larry the Locksmith had jumped onto the side of the Cube in an attempt to open the door, but the door was too hot and burned his hands. As kids ran out of the store to escape the fire and the falling skeletons, Sarah grabbed Harry.

"You have to do something!" she screamed.

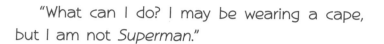

"What can I do? I may be wearing a cape, but I am not *Superman*."

"No, you're better than Superman — because you are real. Use your magic, Harry Moon. Save your enemy."

"You're right," he agreed.

She reached down and turned his face to hers. "Abracadabra," she whispered to him. In her hand was the almond-wood wand.

"Thanks," he said, grabbing it and running toward the Cube.

"Be careful!" Sarah shouted.

Getting to Titus was not as easy as Harry had thought. The crowd was still running, the ceiling was on fire, and the showroom was filling with smoke. Taylor Dingham, the school's best linebacker, clobbered Harry in the chin with his right elbow, unable to see as he ran for his own life. As Harry fell to the floor, his wand went flying. Reaching blindly through the smoke, he searched for the wand.

"Wand to me," he commanded, not knowing what else to do. And there it was — tight in his fingers! The wand's obedience to him gave him confidence. As he opened his arms, with the wand in his right hand, Harry cried, "Abracadabra!"

He did not know how he got there, but he was on top of the fallen Cube. He had his hand on what had to be the handle. But the handle was cold to his touch. He waved the wand in front of his eyes, and he could see past the smoke. He yanked on the handle, but it did not budge.

He waved the wand over his hand. He again reached for the handle, but it had disappeared. In its stead was a hole. He reached inside the opening and pulled at the surface of the door. In his hand, the thick metal became tin. He peeled it back from the Cube as if he was opening a can of sardines.

He could hear Titus's cough. Harry

gasped. "He's alive!" he said to himself. He stepped into the Cube, thinking of Titus's mean behavior to so many. Harry thought of Titus's own cruel acts to him — especially that terrible assault on the sidewalk on Nightingale Lane. Harry hesitated, even though Titus was crying — calling for help.

"He must be worth saving," Harry thought. "Otherwise, my magic couldn't work. Right?"

"Right!" said the voice of Rabbit.

"There must be some good in him, right?" Harry debated again.

"There is good in everyone," Rabbit's voice said, "but some people just don't know how to find it."

"I'm right here," said Titus's faint voice from behind a smashed LED screen.

"Be right there," Harry assured him as he approached the groaning. He had to crawl to get to him.

Titus looked up at the screen in front of him. Rising above the screen like a morning sun on the horizon was Harry Moon.

A coughing Titus looked disbelievingly at the boy in the smoky air.

"But I cut your hair off," said Titus, gasping for a breath of good air.

"It grows quickly," Harry replied. "Are you okay?"

"I think so."

Titus rubbed his soot-covered eyelids with his hands. He lifted his eyes back to Harry.

"Who are you, anyway?" Titus asked.

"Just a guy with some magic," Harry replied.

After the endless questions from the Sleepy Hollow Police and Fire Departments, Harry was free to go. Stepping out of Chillie Willies' administration office, Harry walked down the corridor.

The showroom was devastated. The once colorful shop was as grey and hollow as a cave. Everyone was gone except for some firefighters checking for embers. Maintenance folk were sweeping up ashes and debris.

194

Crossing the floor, Harry could not help but think how much trouble his classmates were in. He was at the double doors of the entrance, when he heard a, "Hey!"

"Hey," he said softly. He froze in midstride. "I cannot believe you waited for me."

"No prob," said Sarah, as she rose from her folding chair by the wall. "I drove ... remember? My truck doesn't leave anybody behind."

Harry turned to see her moving through the shadows of the cavernous showroom. As she came closer, the streetlights from outside illuminated her scarves and face. The bangles on her wrists shone.

"A truck doesn't have a diadem," he said. He pulled over a small wooden box from the charred counter.

"What are you doing?" she asked as she reached him.

He stood on the box while she laughed.

"What are you doing, you big goof?" she asked, her face now flushed. He was very close now. And for the first time, he could see her eye to eye.

"Straightening your diadem," he said. He reached out, and arranged the golden tiara with the veil in her blond hair. His hands stayed there a little too long, but she didn't seem to mind.

Then he looked at her, gathering the strands of hair away from her face.

"Someone once said to me that time changes everything."

"Uh huh," she murmured.

"Sometimes that can happen all in a single moment."

She closed her eyes as Harry leaned in to kiss her on the lips. He could not believe he was doing it.

196

As wonderful as he imagined it might be — it was that and more.

Again, he may have stayed there a little too long, but she didn't seem to mind. Because when he pulled his lips from hers, she smiled.

"Abracadabra," she whispered.

Harry smiled. "Abracadabra!"

197

198

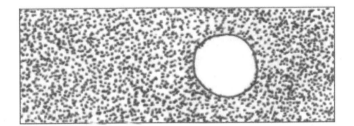

MONDAY

N o one likes Monday — and that included Harry Moon. He dreaded going to class ... especially on *that* Monday. Everyone would want to rehash the events of the party at Chillie Willies and who got into what kind of trouble and for how long.

Due to the fire at Chillies, the Selectmen and Town Council convened on Sunday for a special sentencing of the forty kids who admitted they were involved in the "Haunted Cube Incident." These included Bailey Wheeler, Declan Dickinson and Hao Jones.

The sheriff, firefighters, teachers, and half the town were there to decide what to do with the kids. The dramatists at Sleepy Hollow Middle School talked "jail time." The athletes discussed "controlled hazing." The moderates won with <u>detention</u>. It was for six weeks ... *every* afternoon during school and *every* Saturday.

A lot of the perpetrators breathed a sigh of relief that the discipline did not involve a trip to Juvie. This included Clooney Mackay. It was his dad's laptop that burned in the fire, so his dad whacked him silly. Clooney had the welts from the buckle strap to prove it. But as far as anyone was concerned, those welts happened in the "mayhem of the Haunted Cube Incident."

When Harry witnessed the lies that Clooney was telling everyone about his welts, Harry thought about how unfair life could be. Rabbit was right. These were troubled times. "Maybe there will always be trouble," thought Harry. "So why not try and be a hero?"

As Harry walked to school that morning,

he thought how fortunate he was to have a mom and dad who maybe didn't always *seem* to *like* him, but always *loved* him. He was fortunate to have a dad who never hit him, and whose worse fault was to make silly silk screens of Harry's sometimes stupid sayings and pass them out to his friends ... like "No more training wheels for me" or "I wear sunscreen even though I am a Moon."

When Harry got to homeroom, everyone was already in their seats — highly unusual. Even Clooney Mackay and Bailey, who always walked with Harry but "had to get to school early," were in their assigned seats. Harry sat down, and Miss Pryor, also his homeroom teacher, closed the door. She walked to the front of the classroom and stood behind her desk and next to her bust of Shakespeare, "the Genius," as she called him.

"Students, as you know, I oversaw the Scary Talent Show this fall as I always do. On Saturday night, everyone did well, but our Harry Moon was exceptional — not only because of his talents, but because of his strength of character in the way he handled the unfortunate technical ruling regarding his performance. I think we should give him a round of applause."

202

One by one, each student stood. There were Bailey and Clooney...and there was Titus. As they turned, Harry finally got it!

"Geesh," Harry thought. "One day I am going to get my dad for all this stuff." Each student was wearing a custom silk-screened tee with *DO NO EVIL* — courtesy of the Moon garage.

As he walked out of homeroom, Titus headed over to him.

"Harry, I just want to thank you for what you did."

"No sweat," Harry said, as he walked down the corridor to his first class. He felt a tad uncomfortable as Titus was right by his side.

"Also, I want to apologize for being so terrible to you for these past eight years."

"Nine years. Don't forget kindergarten!"

"Nine years then. I am sorry. I really am. Someone told me that when you almost die, you can have an epiphany. So I was reading about Abraham Lincoln and his sad story."

"Titus, Abraham Lincoln died from the shot ... ."

WAND - PAPER - SCISSORS

"Yeah, I know, Harry. I meant earlier. You know what Abraham Lincoln said?"

"What did he say, Titus?"

"What's the best way to get rid of an enemy?"

204

"I don't know."

Lincoln said, "The best way to get rid of an enemy is to make him your friend," Titus explained.

"I like that," Harry said. "Just don't tell my dad. Otherwise, we will all be wearing that on a T-shirt."

In that moment, everything changed for both Harry and Titus. Now the ghouls and ghosts and the Headless Horseman were scarier than their classmates at Sleepy Hollow Middle School.

"That's what you did to me. I was your enemy, but you treated me like a friend. One day, I hope we can be friends, Harry."

"Let's work on it. Let's start today," Harry suggested. "In our little spooky town of Sleepy Hollow, there's plenty of trouble, so let's hang together."

206

AUTHOR'S NOTES

I love Harry Moon. I love everything about him. I love his name. I love his magic. And most of all, I love his courage.

I was never the most popular kid in school. I spent a lot of my time in a barn when I was in middle school taking care of my rabbits. I think I was always a little bit on the outside.

Maybe that's why I relate to Harry so much. He has what it takes to stand up for what is right and isn't afraid to do the hard thing, even as an outsider. That's pretty cool. Of course, he also gets to kiss the prettiest girl in the room, which is not too shabby.

In life, we need a real friend like Rabbit. There is a lot of value in knowing someone who is wise, who can help you through the tough times. That's the point, I think, of these amazing adventures — life is better when you've got a friend who can help point the way.

I am happy that you have decided to come along with me in these amazing adventures of Harry Moon. I would love for you to let me know if there are any fun ideas you have for Harry in his future stories. Go to harrymoon. com and let me know.

208

See you again in the next adventure of Harry Moon!

MARK ANDREW POE

The Adventures of Harry Moon author Mark Andrew Poe never thought about being a children's writer growing up. His dream was to love and care for animals, specifically his friends in the rabbit community.

Along the way, Mark became successful in all sorts of interesting careers. He entered the print and publishing world as a young man and his company did really, really well.

Mark became a popular and nationally sought-after health care advocate for the care and well-being of rabbits.

Years ago, Mark came up with the idea of a story about a young man with a special connection to a world of magic, all revealed through a remarkable rabbit friend. Mark worked on his idea for several years before building a collaborative creative team to help bring his idea to life. And Harry Moon was born.

209

In 2014, Mark began a multi-book print series project intended to launch *The Adventures of Harry Moon* into the youth marketplace as a hero defined by a love for a magic where love and 'DO NO EVIL' live. Today, Mark continues to work on the many stories of Harry Moon. He lives in suburban Chicago with his wife and his 25 rabbits.

BE SURE TO READ THE CONTINUING AND
AMAZING ADVENTURES OF HARRY MOON

FIVE STARS FOR HARRY MOON!

★★★★★

"I am a grandparent. I knew ahead of time that these books were aimed at younger readers but I could not resist and thank goodness for that! This is one of the best books I have read in a long time. Certainly the most fun books I have read in ages. I read the whole thing in one day."
— *Seattle, Washington*

"Harry Moon would be a great book for middle school teachers to assign their students to read. Its a very creative fun story that the kids everywhere will love. The book encourages strong morals and values. Amazing story and can't wait to read the next book."
— *Springfield, Illinois*

"Great coming of age story for the whole family to enjoy! I have been reading it at bedtime with my eight year old daughter, she loved it, can't wait for the next book. This blows away *Wimpy Kid*."
— *Dallas, Texas*

"The cover and illustrations throughout are humorous and likely to attract a child's initial attention to the book. Kids will relate to Harry Moon—being bullied, being picked last for sports, being too short, being annoyed by a know-it-all little sister and having a name that provokes teasing. Even the potty-mouth, trash talking seems authentic. What kid hasn't wished for the ability to wave a wand and make rabbits fly, get the best of a bully, or be hailed as a hero."
— *Colorado Springs, Colorado*

"Harry himself describes his magic this way: "It's strange being visitors to this world. As hard as we try, we don't quite get it. We still see glimpses of something more—a deeper magic. I see it in my little brother's eyes. I see it in the beauty of the sunrise. But as hard as any of us try, we don't ever have all the answers. So to-night…I hope to take you through a doorway into that wonder that lies behind the sunrise." I think C.S. Lewis would have enjoyed this book."
— *Upland, Indiana*

"That's right, Harry is a thirteen-year-old magician with a not quite so ordinary assistant. Harry's side-kick is a rabbit, an invisible Harlequin bunny (or is he invisible, uhm) who helps him out. An engaging, fun story on the surface but chock full of the deep things all kids Harry's age grapple with, including how to handle a scissors-yielding bully determined to keep Harry from winning the school talent show."
— *Aimes, Iowa*

"I don't usually read the books I buy for my sons, but I could not help reading this one. I loved it. A wonderful story, a strong bond between mother and son, a caring family and a young man named Harry I am anxious for my sons to get to know. Just perfect."
— *St. Louis, Missouri*

"Just like C.S. Lewis's *Chronicles of Narnia* show us what evil looks like and makes reference to "good magic", so too does Harry Moon. The setting is spooky and there is an evil villain with bad motives. Yet, as the preface states, "Harry has been chosen by the powers of light to do battle against the mayor and his evil consorts." Go Harry, go."
— *Dayton, Ohio*

"Finally, it is encouraging to see someone writing books for middle school kids with a more heroic young character, rather than a "wimp" or a "dork."
— *Milwaukee, Wisconsin*

"Harry's adventures remind me of *Diary of a Wimpy Kid* except this story has a message about character. It opens up dialogue between parents and children that is important as they giggle and admire Harry as he faces hard things in school and life. That's a win-win for everyone."
— *Pottstown, Pennsylvania*

"I enjoyed this book of childhood angst and joy as much as I would have years ago. I can relate to Harry Moon and am positive he will keep young readers spellbound as well. Harry embodies all that kids today need to hear, want to hear, and already experience. Parents will not have to coax their young readers to finish this book... the book itself will take care of that. I can't wait for the Harry's next adventure. Read, children, read!"
— *Phoenix, Arizona*

"An eccentric cast of characters, which includes a magical rabbit, annoying bully, crazy family, spooky town and loyal friends, make Harry Moon a ten. Every teen struggles with acceptability and fitting in. Harry shows how to do it while "doing no evil". Can Harry use magic for good and resist the temptations that come with it? Great lessons of fighting the urge to be mean back and how to be happy with who you are make this a good read."
— *Atlanta, Georgia*

"A wonderful story, love all the names in the Moon family. This story is throwback to a time when stories inspired its readers to become heroes. I just love it."
— *Stockton, California*

"Harry would have changed his name if he could, but he is named after his dad's best friend who died saving dad's life so there is no chance that will happen. Lucky for us. This is the best character I have brought into our home in quite some time."
— *Lincoln, Nebraska*

"I wish I had a pal like Rabbit when I was growing up, or when my boys were growing up. Come to think of it, maybe I did. Underneath the imaginative fun of Harry Moon is a simple story of faith. Mary Moon, Harry's mom, says it best later in the book. "Harry," she tells her son, "there will always be trouble in the world so there will always be room for heroes."
— *Newark, New Jersey*

VISIT HARRYMOON.COM FOR everything HARRY, HONEY & THE LATEST NEWS

JOIN THE HARRY MOON BOOK CLUB

Every 12 month subscriber receives each of these benefits:

1. **SIX hardcover editions** of *The Amazing Adventures of Harry Moon*. That's a new book delivered every two months. *(3 books for 6 mo. subscribers)*

2. **SIX free e-book versions** of each new book (downloaded using our included Harry Moon smart phone and tablet app. *(3 books for 6 mo. subscribers)*

3. **SIX free audio versions** of each new book (downloaded using our included Harry Moon smart phone and tablet app. *(3 books for 6 mo. subscribers)*

4. Your first book is delivered in a beautiful **Harry Moon "cigar style" Collectables Box**.

5. **Wall posters** of Harry, Rabbit and all their friends are on the inside of each book's dust jacket—images straight from the Sleepy Hollow Portrait Gallery.

6. The very popular and useful **monogramed drawstring backpack** from the Sleepy Hollow Outfitters store.

7. From the Sleepy Hollow Magic Store a **pouch of magical fragrances** transporting you to the town's aromas.

8. The large 15" x 21" **Fun Map of Sleepy Hollow**—takes you everywhere around town.

9. A **special edition** of the *Sleepy Hollow Gazette*, including a welcome from the mayor and stories about the upcoming books and not-to-miss events. PLUS, you receive monthly editions of the *Sleepy Hollor Gazette* via email and the app.

10. Plus, if you choose, the Keepsake Box will also include the **golden Sleepy Hollow Outfitters carabiner**. Very handy.

11. And a second optional choice is to include the very cool **Harry Moon monogramed knit beanie**.

Total value of this package - $215 (plus optional items 10 and 11)